Nightmare In The Shadows

Stephanie Brown

Nightmare In The Shadows

Nightmare Series Book 1

Cover by Amanda Walker PA & Designs

Editing by Jimmilee Prouty & James Brown

Formatting by James Brown

Copyright © 2016 Stephanie Brown

Printed in the United States Of America

Third Edition

All rights reserved.

This is a work of fiction. All characters and situations appearing in this work are fictitious. Any resemblance to real persons, living or dead, or personal situations is purely coincidental.

Dedication

I dedicate this book to a man who was always supportive and loving. A man who believed I could achieve any dream I had. He encouraged me to never give up, and to always stand up for my beliefs. My grandfather, Gentry Brown, was the kindest, sweetest, and the most honorable man I have ever met. He loved everyone no matter what. I miss him every day, and hope he's looking down on me with a smile.

I also dedicate this book to my father. James Brown is a man who loves me unconditionally, and supports me as I follow my dream of being an author. I'm sorry for the emotional roller coaster ride I have thrown at you, Dad. You are my biggest supporter. My only hope is that I make you proud. Thank you for being the best father a girl can have.

Contents

Chapter One   1

Chapter Two   9

Chapter Three   25

Chapter Four   33

Chapter Five   41

Chapter Six   55

Chapter Seven   71

Chapter Eight   89

Chapter Nine   95

Chapter Ten   109

Chapter Eleven   121

Chapter Twelve   131

Chapter Thirteen   147

Chapter Fourteen   163

Chapter Fifteen   183

Chapter Sixteen   199

Chapter Seventeen   215

Acknowledgements   231

About The Author   233

Chapter One

My name is Brooke Stevens. I'm 26 and work for a small newspaper in Kansas City, Missouri. My life was normal until, while visiting my father, the unthinkable happened. The small town where I grew up was turned upside down when the bodies of six murder victims were found by a jogger in a field outside of town. In just a matter of minutes our town went from small and cozy, with no one afraid to leave their front doors unlocked, to a town who barricaded themselves in. They went from trusting their neighbors to being afraid that someone they trusted for so long was a serial killer. No one trusted anyone. Security systems were installed, locks were changed, and kids no longer played outside. Although I was on vacation, my boss called and asked me to investigate the story. I wasn't thrilled about investigating, and writing about a serial killer, but it was my job. I reluctantly headed out to interview the police, and the woman who found the bodies. This is where my story starts, and it is where my life changed forever.

To fully understand my story and how it truly affected me and the small community of Brines, Missouri, I must start by telling you more about the town. Brines has a population of about 2,081. It's a small town that still has the small town feel. People would wave as their cars passed one another, kids always felt safe walking to school or hanging out with friends, and everyone helped each other when needed. Brines only had two stop lights that were put in place due to the highway going through town. It was a town that still said Merry Christmas instead of Happy Holidays. There were eleven churches that filled up every Sunday. Everyone was always happy and had smiles on their faces.

On the night of August 29th a young jogger discovered the bodies of 6 victims in her neighbor's field. When my boss called and assigned me to cover the story, my vacation was cut short. Reluctantly, I gathered a few pens, a notebook, grabbed my keys and headed to the scene. I was met by 29 year old Officer Logan Galloway. I showed him my press pass, flashed him a smile, and asked if he had any information he could share.

"I can't talk about an open case, I'm sorry," he kindly explained.

I looked up at him with a sweeter smile. "I know there has to be some information you can give me. I'm not asking for names. If you can't tell me anything, can you tell me who can?"

Just as he was about to answer Detective David James, a good friend of the family, walked over to us, and with a smile leaned over to give me a hug. "How are you doing Brooke? I heard you were in town on vacation. You know most people go somewhere tropical for vacation. They don't hang out at crime scenes." He laughed his deep belly laugh.

"You know me Uncle David. I never do what everyone else does, that's too boring. Besides my boss wants me to get some information and send it to him," I half smiled. "I wish I didn't have to be here. You know this freaks me out. Since the unsolved murder of my mother 10 years ago, these types of things aren't easy for me. I know you can't give out too much information, but any little bit will be greatly appreciated."

He wrote something on a piece of paper and handed it to me. "Maybe we can meet for coffee later and catch up. It's been awhile since we last talked. I have to get back to work. I'll be done here in a few hours. It's great to see you. Make sure you stop by and visit my wife while you're in town. Have a great night sweetie."

I gave him a hug, and let him get back to work. As he walked away I read what he wrote. Meet me at Sweet and Salty Eats off of highway 63 at 11 pm. Where we met early in the morning before we'd all go fishing or hunting. I really hoped he was going to give me some inside information. I had a few hours left before the meeting, so I hopped in my Escape and headed over to see his wife, Elizabeth. It had been 3 years since I last saw her. We did, however, talk on the phone at least once a month. She kept me up to date on all the local gossip. I decided to call before stopping by due to the recent murders. I knew that it might be a bad idea to just stop by. Elizabeth was so happy to hear my voice and was excited to have someone there with her.

As I pulled into the driveway of their small rock home, I was flooded with memories of my childhood. Spending my weekends with Aunt Elizabeth learning how to cook new things and bake all kinds of sweets. Neither my mom nor my dad could cook or bake. We ate out almost every night. That is until I was 15 when I started cooking dinner at least 5 nights a week. I took what I learned from Aunt Elizabeth and tried to teach my parents, but failed miserably at it. I think they just didn't want to learn. I didn't mind cooking though. It made me feel like I was more helpful to my parents. It was one less thing for them to worry about after a hard day's work. It made me smile to recall the memories as I walked up to the door. I didn't have to knock since Aunt Elizabeth was waiting by the window and watching for me to arrive. I was greeted with the biggest hug, and rushed inside, so she could lock the doors up tight. I could see the fear in her aging eyes.

"It's so great to see you," she cried as she hugged me again. "It's been far too long. You need to visit more often. I know your father misses you greatly."

"I'm glad I could finally get some time off to come down for a visit. However, in all this excitement, I am now working on my only vacation in three years." I sat on the couch and tried to relax a bit. "You know I would visit more often if I could. The two of you are like my second family. You taught me how to cook many different meals and bake your award winning pies. You also helped me deal with my mother's murder. Why don't we talk about what you've been up to lately," I suggested trying to change the subject away from death. "Are you still working part time for the diner making pies and cakes?"

"We should go to the kitchen and have some coffee. You look exhausted," she replied and motioned for us to head into the kitchen. "I am still baking for them, but not just pies and cakes. I now bake cookies and once a week I go in and cook catfish for the Sunday night special. Apparently, no one else in town makes it as good as I do. My secret for great catfish is to not use catfish at all." She laughed as she finished filling the coffee pot and hit start. "I guess David will want me to stop doing that until they catch this serial killer. I'm ok with that though. I can still do my baking and have him drop it off for me."

"Besides baking and frying up the world's best catfish, what have you been up to? What's the latest gossip in town? Who is unmarried and pregnant? Who is being cheated on?" I asked excited to talk about anything but murder.

She grabbed a couple coffee mugs and some sugar,

trying to stall. "Well, I'm not up to much else since baking takes up most of my time. Oh! You remember Sharon Douglas?" I nod. "Well she came in to the diner two weeks ago crying and looking like she hadn't slept in days. Being my usual caring self I asked her what was wrong. She told me her husband left her for their 19 year old babysitter."

"Are you serious? Wait, wasn't their babysitter Jacob McKenzie? I bet she was devastated," I said in total shock. "I dated her husband when I was in high school. He was always so handsy. Poor Sharon, but good for him. I'm glad he was honest with himself."

"That's not all," she said as she poured our coffee. "He filed for divorce and accused Sharon of being mentally abusive to their two children, and he wants full custody. I think I hurt her feelings when I didn't take her side. She's always yelling at those kids and calling them names. I can't approve of that kind of treatment towards young children. A week later he came in and asked me if I would testify on his behalf in court. I told him I would, and now Sharon's mom is calling me a traitor. I just think those children would have a better life living with a parent who loves and encourages them. You know what I mean?"

We talked for a couple more hours and drank our coffee. It was a lot of fun and a great distraction, until my phone rang. It was, of course, my boss wanting to know what I found out. I explained that they weren't releasing any information, but I knew the lead detective on the case and was on my way to meet him for coffee. I said I would email him any information I could get. I hugged Elizabeth and said my goodbyes, then headed to the diner.

I got there a half hour early, so I sat in a corner booth and glanced at the menu trying to decide if I should order or wait for Uncle David to arrive. By the time I made a decision he was already walking into the diner. I waved him and his fellow officer to the table. "Great," I thought. "Now I'll never get any information from him." I just smiled as they took their seats.

"Hello Uncle David. Who is your good looking friend?" I asked trying not to stare at the handsome young officer.

"Hello Brooke. This is Officer Logan Galloway. He wants to work for the FBI, so I thought I would let him help me out on the case. I figured it would be a great experience so that maybe he could get ahead of the game when he leaves for training in a month or so." He looked at Officer Galloway and smiled. "We can't tell you much about the case until we have more information to go on, but I have some information to give you before anyone else. The other reporters won't get any information until the press conference tomorrow morning."

"It is nice to meet you Officer Galloway. Don't listen to my Uncle and the evil things he tells you about me," I retorted with a mischievous grin before turning back to Uncle David. "Any information you have is good. Thank you for this and I hope you won't get in any trouble. That's the last thing I want."

Officer Galloway excused himself saying he was going to the counter to order everyone something to eat. We smiled and nodded. "Don't forget cheese on her fries!" David shouted after him.

"So far all I can say is that while a jogger was running along DD Highway she decided to cut through her neighbor's field and stumbled upon 6 dead bodies." He cleared his throat, and tried to continue.

"Take your time. I know this isn't easy. Death never is." I grabbed his hand to reassure him that it would be okay.

"The young woman who found the bodies was taken to the station to give her statement. It was very odd. She acted frightened, but it looked as though she was hiding something. She didn't act like someone should when they find any dead bodies, let alone six of them. We could only identify one of them. She went missing around July 29th. We only know this because her family contacted us a month ago to report her missing. I can't give you the name at this time. All I can say is that we know she was not from around here. She was just passing through town. That's all the information I have at this time." He gave me a half smile and continued, "Now let's talk about what you have been up to the last few months."

"Thank you for the information tonight. It may not be much, but it will be helpful enough to get my boss off my back."

Officer Galloway joined us at the table, followed by the little red haired waitress carrying our food. "I got extra cheese for the fries and burgers for all of us. I hope that's okay."

"I love the burgers here. They are so greasy and cheesy. You can't get 'em like this anywhere else. Thanks Officer Galloway," I explained with a big grin on my face.

"No problem. Detective James gave me a heads up on what you would want on the way here. He figured it would be a good idea for me to not be at the table when the two of you talked just in case he gets in any trouble."

"Always looking out for others. He's the best uncle in the world."

"You're going to make me blush, Brooke. So what have you been up to?" Uncle David asked embarrassed.

"The usual boring stuff. All I do is work, sleep, and work some more. I never have time to go out and do anything fun anymore. While other people my age are having fun or raising children, I keep busy with my work at the paper and writing articles for various magazines. Even though I'm working on my vacation, I still can't complain," I admitted.

"Maybe you can find some time to go out and have a little fun while in town. Who knows, maybe you'll decide you like it better here and move back. It would be nice to have you come to the house more often. Elizabeth misses you so much. She has no one to bake with anymore."

"I don't see that happening, but you never know. It is great seeing my dad again. If my boss continues being a total douche bag, you just might get your wish."

We finished our food and said goodbye. When I got to my dad's, I wrote a small article and emailed it to my boss. Then I sent him a text so he would know to check his inbox. He replied to my text, but I wasn't in the mood for a conversation so I closed it out. I then settled into bed with a good book and fell asleep before I even finished the first paragraph.

Chapter Two

The next morning I woke because my cell phone was ringing. I looked at the caller id and saw that it was an unknown number. I decided I might as well answer it since it already disturbed my sleep. "Hello. May I ask who is calling?"

"This is Echo Shay. I got your number from Detective James." she paused for a moment. "I told him I would give you an exclusive interview after the press conference in a few hours. I hope that's ok?"

"That's perfect," I said with a nervous feeling in the pit of my stomach. "Just let me know where and when you would like to meet. I'm free anytime this afternoon."

"Can we meet at Sweet and Salty Eats about 1 o'clock? It's a public place, but still on the private side that time of day."

"That will be perfect. I'll see you then." At least it's in a public area I thought to myself as I hung up the phone.

I fixed a quick breakfast and caught up a bit with my dad before he headed off to work. I got my shower, prepared for the day, and checked my email to see if my boss had emailed me back and found nothing. I sent him one to let him know about the press conference at noon and my scheduled interview with the woman who found the bodies. After sending the email, I gathered my stuff and headed off to the police department for the press conference.

I was the first reporter to arrive, so I went in and scoped out a spot right in front. As I sat and waited for the others to arrive and the conference to begin, I checked my email again, sent out a few text messages, and before I knew it the room was packed full. Uncle David entered the room and began talking. I took notes and used my recorder.

"Ladies and Gentlemen of the press, I am here to explain the details of last night's horrifying events. As you already know a jogger stumbled upon a mass grave containing six bodies last night. After taking her statement and hours of questioning, we were able to rule her out as a suspect. We then had a few officers talk to the owner of the land the bodies were found on. After a short time of talking with her, a search warrant was issued for her house and property. Upon investigation, several officers found what appeared to be a large room used for torture. A more extensive investigation was done and blood residue was found on all of the floors, walls, and a large table. Officers found multiple tools used in the torture and death of the victims. The woman was promptly taken into custody. At this time we have only been able to identify one of the victims. She was 21 year old Linda Garret of Edgewater, Colorado. She was visiting her cousin last month when she disappeared. I'm sorry that is all the information we have at this time. We will not be taking any questions while the investigation is still ongoing. The Brines Police Department will try and have another press conference when we have more information. Thank you all."

The room erupted with reporters yelling out questions, hoping to get more answers. Uncle David left the room without answering any of them. Knowing there was nothing else I grabbed my recorder from the podium and headed to my car. On the way to the diner my mind raced with so many questions. I know who used to own the property where the bodies were found, but couldn't picture 76 year old Emma Bradley as a serial killer. She must have moved or passed away. I hoped my interview with Echo would give me some insight as to who lived there. After all, she did live next door to the alleged serial killer. I arrived at the diner and saw a strange young woman with blue hair waving for me to join her. All I could think was that it couldn't get any weirder than it already was. That is until I sat down and noticed her yellow contact lenses. "I think I just walked into the Twilight Zone," I thought to myself.

I took my seat, and introduced myself before waving the waitress over and ordering some lunch. "Hello I'm Brooke. It's nice to meet you, but I'm curious as to why you chose me for an exclusive interview. I only work for a small paper." I looked at her confused, and finally remembered to start my recorder. "Don't get me wrong. I am grateful for this opportunity, it just confuses me that I'm the one you chose."

She looked at me and smiled. "I chose you because we went to school together. Though we didn't hang out and I was a few grades behind you, I still know you and feel more comfortable with you. Besides I don't like talking to strangers. Just because I look and dress differently, doesn't mean I like the attention. All I ask is that you please omit my name from the article you write. Where would you like me to start?"

"Just start at the beginning. I'll try to save any questions I may have until you are finished." I smiled to let her know she could trust me. "If at any time you are uncomfortable, feel free to stop. I want you to know that you don't have to talk about anything you don't want to talk about."

"Okay! Last night I was jogging home from the gym like I do five nights a week. I was getting tired so I decided to cut through my neighbor's fence and take a shortcut through her field. I didn't make it that far when I tripped over a large rock and fell into a hole. At first I thought that maybe she was burying rocks in the field. She was always complaining about them and not being able to afford to move them. I remembered that in April she had rented a backhoe and started digging a large pit like hole in that area. That's why I assumed it was rocks. I pulled out my phone to use as a light because I didn't want to fall again and hurt myself anymore than I already had. As I shined my light into the hole I saw several big rocks. When I was getting up I noticed some of the dirt had been disturbed by my fall, and there was a hand sticking out of it." She paused and took a deep breath before continuing. "At first all I could do was scream, but after a few minutes I carefully climbed out of the hole, trying my best to not disturb anything else. I then called 911 and told them what I found and where I was. When the police arrived, I was quickly taken to the station to give my statement. I spent several hours being questioned." She paused again to eat some of her food. "All I could think was, 'No wonder everyone hates joggers. We're always the ones who find the bodies.' You know what I mean?" she let out a small chuckle that threw me off guard.

"I know what you're thinking. How did I not hear the screams of the victims? How did I miss my neighbor dumping bodies in the field?" she took a drink of her coffee and continued. "That's easy. I live alone and work from home. I love music and always have it blasting from my computer. I have wireless speakers all over my house so I can play music in every room. My neighbors aren't too close as many of them are farmers. So I play my music as loud as I can. That's probably why I never heard anything. As for not seeing the bodies being dumped, I guess that is because I rarely leave the house at night. I doubt any bodies were dumped during the day. I jog to the gym at 4 pm, work out for 30 minutes, and then I jog home. Last night I got to the gym late because I stopped by a friend's house to fix her computer. That's basically everything I know. If you have any questions I will try to answer them the best I can."

We took a short break to finish our meals. I took the time to think of a few questions. "Who lives in that house now? Last I knew 76 year old Emma Bradley was the owner."

"Emma passed away just about a year ago. She left the house to her daughter, Melissa. A month after taking over the house, Melissa was in a horrible accident. She has been in a coma ever since. Naturally her daughter Clara took over the house."

"Did you know Clara very well? Were you friends or just acquaintances?" I needed more information on Clara.

"I didn't know her very well. She was the quiet type. I saw her around town and occasionally I would see her when I went to get my mail, but we never really talked. I did know Emma pretty well. She used to make me a casserole once a week and come over to eat dinner with me. I think she was lonely. We often talked about how she missed her daughter. She once told me that her daughter ran away from home at sixteen because her husband was abusive. She would talk to her on the phone, until Mr. Bradley passed away. It was then that she was reunited with Melissa. Melissa's boyfriend was controlling and abusive. Emma was upset by this and tried to get her daughter to leave him. Long story short, Melissa had Clara when she was twenty four. She stayed with her boyfriend until Clara was about ten. The final straw for Melissa was when her boyfriend pushed Clara down a flight of stairs, and then repeatedly kicked her in the stomach. That's all

Emma ever told me. Maybe that's what caused her to end up like she is. Who knows these days?"

"So there were never any signs that she was a murderer?"

"Not anything that I ever noticed. Like I said, I barely knew Clara. She may have been a neighbor, but she was still basically a stranger. I'm sorry I don't have any more information."

"I have one last question then I'll let you get on with your day. Do you know if she had a boyfriend or someone who may have helped her with any of the killings?"

"I've never seen her with anyone before, but I suppose it's possible. She doesn't look strong enough to have done it on her own, but looks can be deceiving."

"Thank you so much Echo. This is very helpful." I turned off the recorder. "If you think of anything else, please don't hesitate to give me a call." Echo quietly slipped out of the diner as I paid our bill. I grabbed my recorder and headed out to interview some of Clara's neighbors.

At the first house, the young woman refused to open the door and yelled for me to get off her porch. Frustrated, I moved on to the next house. An older gentleman answered and greeted me with a smile. I recognized him as my high school math teacher. It was nice to see someone from my teen years. I remembered him as the nice yet very strict teacher that treated his class like we were all in the military. I did love his class though.

"Hello Mr. Woods. How have you been?"

"Ms. Stevens, it's wonderful to see you again. Unfortunately I was forced into retirement two years ago. To what do I owe this pleasure?"

"I work for a small paper in Kansas City and would love to ask you a few questions if you don't mind."

"I don't mind at all. Come on in and I'll make us some coffee. Make yourself comfortable please."

"I really appreciate this. No one else wants to talk to me. My article will be pretty short unless I can get more people to talk to me. Any information you can give me will be a big help."

"I'll tell you everything I know." He brought in some coffee and sat in the chair across from me. "Is there anything in particular that you'd like to know?"

"Let's start with what Clara was like in school."

"She kept to herself from what I saw. Although I do remember her getting into a few fights. I think she was looking out for a younger student, but I couldn't tell you the name of the other student. Clara got good grades for the most part. Several times she showed up covered in bruises. I just assumed it was from the fights. That's all I remember from school. My memory isn't the greatest these days. I guess it's why they wanted me gone."

"That's very helpful, and I thank you. What was she like as a neighbor? Was she quiet, or did she like to cause trouble?"

"She was fairly quiet from what I remember. Now that I'm thinking about it, she did have a lot of people going in her house later at night. I never saw any of them leave, but I didn't pay much attention to her. Maybe I should pay more attention to my neighbors from now on. I'm sorry I wasn't more of a nosey neighbor."

"You have nothing to be sorry about. We never know when people will turn bad. I think I have enough information. I have a little more time before I need to head home and cook dinner if you want me to stay and chat for a bit."

"That would be so wonderful, but I actually need to get my nap in before getting ready for a date tonight. You're never too old to find a new love."

"I will go and let you get your nap. Thank you for the coffee and the information on Clara. Enjoy your date tonight." I shook his hand and headed out the door.

I had a little more time before I needed to be home so I tried the next house. This time I was greeted by an angry man with a shotgun. He pointed it at my head and told me to get off his property or else. I slowly turned and ran for my car. I guess he was a little on edge or tired of people trying to get information from him. I finally gave up and headed home.

After I got back to my dad's house and took a minute to relax, I got the roast and some baby carrots out of the fridge and put them into a roasting pan. I cut a few potatoes, added them to the pan, mixed up some spices in water with a can of cream of mushroom soup, poured it over the roast, and put dinner in the oven. I grabbed a can of soda from the fridge, sat in dad's ultra comfy recliner, and turned on the television. After the interview I just needed to relax. I checked my email on my phone and saw one from my boss. He said he wanted an article on the press conference and the interview by 8 pm. He needed it in time to send it out for the morning paper. "There goes my relaxation time," I mumbled to myself. I got up and grabbed my laptop so I could get started right away. While it was loading I grabbed my recorder and started on my article.

My dad got home just as I took a break to check on dinner. "Just in time for dinner Dad, how was your day?"

"It was horrible," he sighed. "All anyone could talk

about was the murders. I hope you had a better day."

I laughed a little too loud. "I'm doing another article on it. So no I did not have a better day than you. I had to go to the press conference, and then I had an exclusive interview with the young woman who found the bodies. It was weird. She didn't cry or freak out while discussing it. She's a little on the weird side with blue hair and yellow contacts. There's something not right about her, but I can't put my finger on it. I also decided to interview a few neighbors. The first yelled through the door to get off her porch. The second was my old math teacher Mr. Woods. He told me everything he remembered. At the third house I was greeted by a man pointing a shotgun at my head. That's when I called it quits. Can we talk about something else tonight please? I still have to finish my article and have it emailed by 8 pm. I need something else to talk about. So, do you have a girlfriend yet?"

He chuckled at my question causing me to burst into laughter with him. "No honey, I still don't have a girlfriend. You know I'm not looking. No one will ever replace your mother. No one can even come close. Is there a special man in your life?"

I fixed our plates as I tried not to laugh. "Touché! No one in my life either. I've been too busy to even think about dating. You see how well my vacation turned out." I looked down at my dinner plate. "I work 7 days a week most of the time. When I do get an odd day off, all I do is sleep. It's the life I chose though. On a good note, besides rent, food, and utilities, I don't spend any money. I have a nice savings set up. I should be able to retire in about five years, move back here, and live comfortably if I want to. Maybe someday I'll retire and write a book. You never know."

We finished dinner, and Dad offered to clean up so I could get back to writing my article. I finished by 7 pm and started working on a quick edit. As I finished my edits, and prepared to send it, my phone rang yet again. This time it was Uncle David.

"Hello, Uncle David. Is everything okay?"

"Yes, I was calling for two reasons. First of all, how did your interview with Echo go? Was she helpful at all?"

"I got enough between the press conference, the interview with Echo, and an interview with a neighbor to get my article done. I was actually getting ready to send it off. What else did you need?"

"It's a big favor," he said and I could hear fear in his voice. "We have been trying to get information from the alleged serial killer, but she is refusing to talk to us unless we have a member of the press in the room. Her lawyer has agreed, but said it needs to be someone local. Local, as in someone from Brines. You're the only reporter of any kind who grew up in this town. I guess what I'm asking is, can you come down to the station and sit in on the interview tomorrow? I know it will be uncomfortable, but it may be the only way we get any information out of her. You will have all rights to use any information for any articles you write. I know it is a lot to ask, but please think about it. We will take a break from questioning her until tomorrow."

"That is a lot to ask. Wow!" I exclaimed. "Let me send in my article and think on it tonight. I will call you in the morning and let you know my answer. Right now I want to catch some shows I missed and get some sleep."

"Thank you for thinking about it. I will talk to you in the morning."

I finished my email and hit the send button. Then I sent a text to my boss so he knew to check his inbox. I poured myself a glass of wine, sat down to watch my shows, and talked some more with my dad.

"What did David want?" he inquired.

"The alleged serial killer is refusing to answer any questions unless they get a reporter from Brines to sit in on the questioning. I just happen to be the only reporter from this small town. Everyone at our local paper is from out of town, so they want me to come in and record everything. I will be able to use any information acquired during the interview in any future articles I write."

"Are you kidding me?" Dad yelled. "That's too dangerous. Did they even think of that? What are they thinking? You can't do this."

"It's not that dangerous. She will be in hand and leg cuffs. There will be police, and Uncle David would never let anything happen to me. Besides, I haven't even made my decision yet. All I did was tell him I would think about it. Please don't get so upset. I promise to give it a lot of thought and consideration before I decide anything."

"I really hope you don't do it. I would worry too much, but I guess you're an adult and can make your own choices in life. I'm asking you to please, don't do this."

"I love you Dad. Why don't you get some sleep? I know you have to be at work early in the morning. I promise to think long and hard about this."

Dad gave in and went to bed. I finished watching my show, rinsed out my wine glass, and headed to my bed to try and sleep. For the first couple of hours all I could do was toss and turn. When I finally fell asleep, I had the worst nightmare. I dreamt that while I was in the room during the interview, a shadowed figure appeared and killed everyone in the room but me. It was a large towering shadow figure. All I could do was sit in my chair frozen. I couldn't scream, run, or even move my head. The shadow figure slowly floated toward me. In that moment, I knew I was a goner. As it reached out to grab my neck, I heard it speak. It spoke in a low deep rumble, "I killed your mother, and I killed your Uncle David. Now I will kill you slowly. I will savor every minute of it." It wrapped its long slender hands around my neck and slowly started to squeeze. At that moment I woke up screaming. I knew it was a dream, yet it still made me cry. I was sobbing uncontrollably by the time my dad ran into my room.

"Are you okay? What happened?"

"It's okay Dad. I just had a bad dream about Mom," I lied. "All this just brings back memories of her murder. Go back to sleep. I promise I'm okay. I'm just going to get a drink of water then go back to sleep."

"I still have nightmares too," he admitted. "If you are sure that you are alright, I'll go get a little bit more sleep before work." He kissed my forehead and headed back to his room.

I got a glass of water, grabbed my book, and curled back up in bed. I never got back to sleep, and I could not concentrate on reading. I gave up and went into the living room to check my email. I replied to a couple of friends who sent emails of concern. They couldn't believe there was a serial killer in such a small town. I assured them that I was safe and working on the story. I promised to send them updates every couple of days. I also had another email from my boss. He said my article was amazing and insightful. He told me to let him know as soon as I had any new information. I decided not to tell him about possibly sitting in on the interview. I wasn't sure yet if I was even going to do it. If I told him, he would tell me I had no choice if I wanted to keep my job. I didn't want or need that kind of pressure. After all, I was already having nightmares. I closed my email and decided to see what was going on with my friends on social media.

The only thing anyone seemed to be talking about was the "Brines Missouri Shadow Killer." I immediately thought of my nightmare. "I can't believe they gave her that name. Why must they give them names? They are just giving the killers the fame they so desire," I told myself. I spent an hour sitting and staring off into space and was startled by my dad coming out of his room to get ready for work. I pretended I had been sleeping.

"Good morning Daddy. I'm so sorry I woke you up last night. I hope you were able to get back to sleep and you aren't too tired today."

"It's okay sweetie. I fell right back to sleep. Did you decide if you are going to sit in on the interview or not?"

"Not yet Dad. I think I'll make my decision after a couple more hours of sleep. Would you like me to make you some breakfast before I lie back down? It's no trouble. I can make you some pancakes while you get your shower."

"No thank you sweetie. I'm meeting a couple guys from work at the diner. I thought you might like to sleep in. Go get some sleep and I will see you when I get home." He kissed me on the cheek and I went back to try and get some more sleep.

I slept for a few hours, and was awakened by the annoying ringing of my phone. I looked at the caller id, and as I suspected, it was Uncle David, but I hadn't even made my decision.

"Hello!" I mumbled.

"Good morning Brooke. I'm sorry to call you again, but I need an answer so we can start the interrogation."

"I'm not sure it's a good idea. I was up most of the night after a horrible nightmare. Why can't this be an easier decision to make? Give me a half an hour to drink some coffee, and I promise to call you back with an answer."

"I think that's a good idea. I know this is hard on you. If you are not up to it, I will try to find someone else. Thank you for at least considering it. I'll talk to you in a bit."

"Talk to you then Uncle David."

I hung up the phone and made some coffee. As I sipped the coffee I thought about the pros and cons of doing this.

Pros:

Get the chance of a lifetime interview.

Amazing article on the inner workings of a young female serial killer.

Chance to move up to a bigger newspaper.

A raise at work.

Cons:

Nightmares of my mother's murder, and what the serial killer did.

Possible danger.

More work, and even less time off. (No more vacations)

Dad will be upset with me.

My list was small and not very helpful. I noticed a text on my phone. It was, of course, my boss. He wanted more information on the situation. He was demanding, and really starting to piss me off. It was that moment when I decided what I wanted to do. I sent my boss a text telling him he was being an asshole and that I quit. I then called Uncle

David.

"Uncle David? I've made my decision. I'll help out in any way I can."

"Thank you so much. This is unconventional, but it's the only way to get her to talk. Last night after we talked, her lawyer called and said she requested you personally. I have no idea why, but I do know we will do everything possible to keep you safe."

"I know you will. I have to admit something else, but you can't tell anyone. I quit my job today. I just can't work for that man anymore. I'm not sure if that will affect Clara's decision or not, but just in case we can keep this to ourselves."

"I guess I can understand, but what will you do for money? How will you pay your bills? Never mind, I know that's none of my business. I'll see you when you get here sweetie. Bring lots of paper in case she decides to let it all out."

"I'll see you in a bit."

I hung up the phone and rushed to get ready for what could be the longest and scariest days of my life. I wasn't really sure what to expect, or how things would go. The one thing I did know was that I was terrified. This could be a great opportunity or the biggest mistake in my entire career. The worst criminal I had ever interviewed was a mugger. He hadn't killed anyone though. I grabbed my stuff and left.

Chapter Three

I walked into the police station full of confidence with a smile on my face. I was determined to make this work. I knew I had a lot to do, but knew this was something I just needed to do. Uncle David and Officer Galloway both greeted me with smiles and looks of thanks. Although I was terrified, I was happy to help in any way I could. I followed them into the small interrogation room. We discussed the dos and don'ts of the interviews. Simple things such as: Don't show any fear. Don't hand her anything, or take anything from her. Do, when possible, ask questions. Do take notes and/or use a recorder. All of these sounded easy, except the not showing my fear. No matter how hard I tried, I couldn't stop shaking. I was about to be face to face with a woman who tortured and killed 6 people that we knew of. Who knew what information she would reveal? I took a final deep breath as Clara Bradley was brought into the room, and chained to the floor and table.

We all sat silent for what seemed like an eternity. I pulled out my first recorder. "May I record this interview please?" I asked as politely as I could.

"That's why you're here. I want you to tell the world my story." She stared at me with an evil grin on her face as I hit play on the recorder. "I want you to be here while I tell my deepest, darkest secrets. I'll tell the 'pigs' what they need to know. After that I want a one on one interview. Just the two of us so we have no distractions. Think you can handle that, or are you too frightened?"

"That sounds like a good idea to me. These assholes will just get in the way." I played along with her evilness. Anything to try and make this interview go as smoothly as possible.

"Now that we have that settled." Uncle David shot me an angry glance after my comment, "Let's get this started. Who were your victims?"

"Straight to the point, I like your style. I'm guessing you didn't find my secret hiding place. The place where I hide my special keepsakes. Oh how I miss my treasures, but that is a story for later." She looked at me as if she were thinking.

"Just get on with it already. We don't have time to waste on you trying to drag this out any further," Officer Galloway barked at her.

"Someone is a little testy today. Just relax and get comfortable. This could take a while. Victim one was Sharon Russell. She had the most beautiful black hair and big chocolate brown eyes. I saw her in the grocery store on May 2nd. I noticed her walking home and offered to give her a ride." She smiled as she recalled the memory. "I did not take her to her house. Instead I talked her into coming over to my house to hang out. She said she was new in town and was looking to make some friends. It was almost too easy. Once back at my house I pretended to drink and kept pouring her more and more glasses of wine. Once she passed out, I took her down to the basement, chained her to the table, and gagged her. The rest is unimportant right now. She was my first, but not my favorite."

"Who was your second victim?" I asked, trying to sound interested.

"Yes, my second victim. That victim was Randy Dugan. I met him at the bar on June 8th. He said he was in town for a family float trip. We drank for a bit and flirted a lot. I didn't see a ring so I asked if he wanted to go back to my place. He was all too eager to take me up on my offer. I guess fat men like him aren't used to women flirting with them. I told him I was a screamer, so my house was a better option than his tiny hotel. Randy seemed like a man who got off on making women scream. I probably did you and all women a favor by killing him." She grinned and let out another evil laugh. "He never got to have any fun. I asked him to get me a bottle of wine from the basement and I pushed him down the stairs. Don't worry it just knocked him unconscious. He lived long enough for me to torture him."

"My third victim was Billy McGowan. I met him in the middle of town on June 27th. He was just taking pictures and documenting our small town. I struck up a conversation with him, told him I locked my keys in my car, and had him give me a ride home. I convinced him to come inside while I grabbed my spare keys. I hit him over the head and, you know the rest."

"Spare us all of the details for now. You can tell that to Brooke during your one on one interview. All we want are names and dates." Uncle David was obviously getting tired of things already.

"Fine!" Clara snapped. "Number four was Kerry Killman on July 18th. Fifth was Linda Garret on July 29th. She almost got away. And my final victim was Lenn Romin on Aug. 19th. He's the one torn to shreds. He was the most fun to watch die. Anything else you pigs need to know?"

"No, that's all we need for now. We will need you to write it down and sign that it is all true. As promised we will make sure the death penalty is off the table. If you will excuse us, we are going to finish our reports, contact relatives, and get some lunch. You may be a murdering bitch, but the laws state we still have to feed you." Uncle David got up and stormed out of the room.

"I'll be in touch with your lawyer to make arrangements for our interview. Thank you for the opportunity." As I picked up my recorder and turned to leave I couldn't believe I thanked a murderer. I walked out of the room and over to David's desk. I looked at him and forced a smile. "Are you going to be ok?"

"I'll be fine. I know she's hiding something. She had to have a partner. Maybe you can get more information out of her. I just couldn't take it anymore." Uncle David shook his head.

"If it will be of any help I can go home and type everything I recorded. You know I will do anything I can to help try and make this easier." I reached for his hand.

"Are you sure this won't be too much for you? I don't want you to do anything you can't handle. I know this must bring up memories of your mother's murder. I know it does for me. I am so sorry I never found her killer. I promise that I will never stop looking." He puts his face in his hands and starts crying.

I put my arm around him to comfort him. "You have done everything possible. Please don't be so hard on yourself. Maybe the reason you can't find the killer is because he/she is already sitting in jail. Let's just worry about this case for now. I need to get home and start dinner. I'll type up the recording after I eat and bring it to you tomorrow. Try and get some sleep tonight. I'll call you in the morning." I gave him a hug and headed back to my dad's house.

By the time I got home, my dad was already there. He had a look of pure anger on his face. I felt as though I should be walking on egg shells. Last time I saw that look was when I was 11 and my best friend Lily and I stole our neighbors' cat and tried to give it a bath. It ripped up the brand new shower curtain, got soap and water all over the house, and peed all over Dad's bed. When we finally caught it, we tried to use my dads' hair clippers to shave it. We got so much fur caught in it that we started a fire. On a good note, other than the cat being very angry and partly bald, it was not hurt at all. The look on my dad's face when he got home and was met by the neighbor terrified me. Then when he saw what the house looked liked and the puddle of water his half melted clippers were in, it was the first and only time I ever got my ass beat. Here I was 26 years old and thought it was going to happen again. A part of me wanted to get in my Escape and drive away as fast as I could. The other part told me to just face the music. It's not like he can ground me anymore.

"Hi Daddy! How was your day?" I tried to act as innocent as I could.

"My day was great until I came home to hear a message on the answering machine that was left for you. Actually it was two different messages. Why did you quit your damn job? Do you just like the idea of being broke and homeless? I love you, but you aren't staying with me rent free. I can barely pay the bills as it is."

"I quit because I was tired of my demanding asshole of a boss. I'm not going to be broke and I can find an apartment here in town. I already told you I have money saved up. I haven't only been working for the paper, but also freelance writing for several magazines. Plus I still have the insurance money from Mom's death. You saved it for my college tuition. Since I got a full scholarship and worked my way through college, I never spent any of it. I live on minimal money being spent and saved everything I could. I don't need to work. I have been living in a small, cheap, crappy apartment. I cook all of my meals and only eat out when it's for business and work covers the bill. Over the last five years I have actually saved a couple million dollars. So please stop treating me like I am a dumb helpless child. Now that that's settled, what else did I do wrong?" I hated yelling at my dad and arguing, but he was treating me like a child. I couldn't deal with it anymore.

"Wait you have how much saved up? Never mind, the second message was from the lawyer of Clara Bradley. He wanted to know when a good time to start the interviews would be. What the hell is he talking about? I thought you weren't going to do this." His look turned from anger to fear and sadness.

"I knew going in today was the only way she would talk. I did it as a favor to Uncle David. Before you go getting your underwear all in a bunch, I want you to know, that he in no way pressured me to do it. He told me I didn't have to do anything I didn't want to do. For some reason she will only talk to me. I knew this would be hard on Uncle David so I agreed to at least one private interview to try and get more information. Don't worry. There will be at least one guard in there at all times and like today she will be chained to the floor and the table and the table is bolted to the floor. The station will make sure the room is 100% safe before they let me in there with her. Her lawyer will also be in the room." I looked my dad in the eyes. "I know what I'm about to say is going to sound completely insane. Dad, I think she knows what happened to Mom. I could be wrong, but shouldn't I at least see what she has to say? I had a friend do some digging. Before I left the police station one of the officers slipped me this file. After I make us some dinner, I will see what it has to say. Please trust that I will be safe."

He looked at me and sighed. "I guess I can't stop you. All I ask is that if you get too scared, or she makes any threats, that you just walk away. I can't lose my daughter. You're all I have left in this world."

"I promise to stay safe. I won't let any harm come to me. What would you like for dinner?"

"Why don't we order a pizza or two? We can read the file together while we wait for it to get here."

"I love that idea. I'll load up my computer and place our order. Do you still like the same old pizza?"

"The usual please and thank you."

I placed the order and we sat on the couch going over the file together. We found out who Clara's father was, and that he was a suspect in my mother's death. He was released when his alibi checked out. His girlfriend and daughter said they were at his house visiting. If I was remembering correctly, my mother died when I was 16, which meant Clara was about 17. I wouldn't think Clara and her mother would visit him after what he did. I could be wrong, but something didn't seem right.

"I was told Clara's father, Victor, pushed her down the stairs and kicked her repeatedly when she was 10 and that's why they left. Why would they visit him or cover for him 8 years later? Something is off here. I can't put my finger on it, but it sounds a little too suspicious. What do you think?"

"I agree that something doesn't sound right. I'm starting to think you're right about Clara. I still don't like the idea, but I'll stop trying to talk you out of it for a little while at least."

Before I could say anything else the door bell rang. I answered the door and luckily it was the pizzas. We sat at the table eating and discussing the file some more. By the time we finished eating, we both agreed I needed to try and find some answers. It could give us the long awaited break in my mother's case. I put away the leftovers, cleaned up the table, and got my recorder and headphones out. I loaded up my laptop and started the long process of typing out the interview with Clara. I figured I would work all night, and call the lawyer back after I turned in my work to Uncle David and got a small nap. I wanted answers, but I wasn't in a huge hurry to listen to her discuss how she killed each of her victims.

Chapter Four

I finished typing everything up around 1:00am and headed off to get a few hours of sleep. When my alarm went off at 8:00am I got up and got ready for the day. I transferred the document to a flash drive and headed off to see Uncle David. When I arrived at the station it was business as usual. Officers were rushing around getting paper work filed, getting ready to go out on patrol, and questioning newly arrested people. I searched the room for Uncle David and found him sitting at his desk looking almost like a corpse. I could tell he hadn't slept in at least a couple of days.

"Good morning sleepy head," I tried to joke.

"Good morning Brooke. How was your night?"

"It was strange. I went home and got into a fight with Dad. We managed to work it out though. Then I read the file Officer Hudson got for me. Something about it just seemed too strange. I'm hoping Clara will be honest and tell me what she knows about my mother's death. I'm not looking forward to hearing how she tortured and killed anyone, but if it will get her to open up and tell me about my mom, I will do it."

"I always thought her dad did it. I could just be blaming him because of how much I hate him though. I'm sorry you have to go through all of this just in hopes of finding the truth about your mom. I would do it, if she would talk to me."

"That's okay. I can handle it. I promise. Before I forget, here's the flash drive with everything typed out for you. I hope it helps."

"It will help so much. Thank you for helping out. The Chief would like to speak to you about a temporary job offer. He knows you started out doing this to help me out and would do it for free, but I think he feels bad having you listen to all the horror and not getting something out of it. I'll take you in to talk to him." He walked me over to a nice sized office and introduced me to his boss. "Chief Parks, this is Brooke Stevens. I will leave the two of you to talk."

Chief Parks reached out to shake my hand. "It's a pleasure to finally meet you. I've heard so much about you. Detective James thinks the world of you. He says that you used to spend a lot of time at his house learning to cook when you were younger."

"That is true. I loved going over there and just hanging out. He was, and still is, my dad's best friend. I have always called him Uncle David. I would do anything for him, even take a bullet. He said you had a job offer. I wanted to let you know that I didn't agree to do this for money. I did it to help get answers. Well, I'm also doing it to possibly study her and write a book."

"The job would only be temporary. Unless you work for the police station you won't be able to talk to Clara or help with anything. It's our policy. I'm sorry. Before you say no, please let me explain the job. You wouldn't have a set schedule. You come and go as you please. We would allow you access to all of the files for this case and if we are right about her, then we will also give you access to your mother's files. I only ask that you take the time to properly think this through."

"I will give it a lot of thought. I need to work on getting my stuff from my apartment in Kansas City and find a place here in Brines. I know my dad loves me, but I think he will get tired of me soon. I'll call you in a few days and let you know what I decide. I thank you for the offer." I shook his hand once again and headed out to say goodbye to Uncle David.

"I've got some things to do and I may need to leave town for a few days. If I go I'll call you when I get back to town. You better get some sleep tonight. Don't make me ground you Uncle David," I yell as I head out to the parking lot, causing the room erupt in laughter. I let out a small giggle and headed to the closest real estate office so I could try and find a house.

I entered the office and introduced myself. We started by looking at some of the properties online. After an hour of searching I decided on a few houses I would like to see in person. We got in the car and headed for the first house. It was a little smaller than I thought it was. It didn't take long for me to ask to see the next one. The second house was only a few doors down so we walked over. It was a little bigger, but still too small, and needed a lot more work than I thought. So we walked back to the car and headed out to house three. This one was outside the city limits on a gravel road. It was an old Plantation style home. As I entered the home, I commented that it had been slightly remodeled. It had the old feel outside, with a slightly more modern inside. I fell in love with the house and said I wanted to put in an offer. We headed back to the office so I could fill out the paper work. The realtor said she would call me as soon as she heard from the family. I headed back to my dad's to get in some much needed relaxation time and make a few calls.

The first thing I did was put my pajamas back on since I couldn't relax unless I was in my favorite clothes. Then I sat back and watched an episode of one of the shows I had saved on Dad's DVR. I pulled out my laptop and started writing an email to send out to all of my friends back in Kansas City.

Hey, it's me.

I know I haven't been very good at keeping in contact lately. I'm sure you miss my daily emails complaining about my jackass boss, wishing I could go on a real vacation, and telling you how my day went. I also know that some of my friends have been worried and freaking out since hearing about the murders in my home town. You can stop worrying. I promise I am doing fine.

I figured I would send out one big mass email to all my friends. I don't feel like typing it out 20 or so times. Yesterday I finally took a big step. I quit my job. That's right, I quit. No more working for a sleazy, slave driver, asshole boss. I feel so free and a lot happier. I also, at the request of the serial killer, sat in on the interview yesterday. She refused to talk unless I was there. I know it's odd and at the time made no sense to me. Since then I have come across information that leads me to believe she may know who murdered my mother. I was offered a temporary job at the Brines Police Department. It will give me access to the case files for the murders, allow me to further interview her, and if proven she knows who killed my mother, I will have access to those files also. I think I am going to take it.

In light of my recent situation, I have also decided to put in an offer on a house. If they accept, I will make arrangements to end my lease at my apartment and come up there to say my see you laters and pack for the move. I know most of you will be upset, but I feel this is what I need and want to do with my life. I promise to visit as often as I can and will have plenty of room for anyone who wants to come down and visit me. Don't be sad, I can finally become the crazy cat lady we all knew I would become. I will send out an email as soon as I know what is going on with the house. For now, I think I will go and take a nice long bubble bath and then possibly a nap. That's right, you can all be jealous now. I get to take naps and you don't. I look forward to hearing from everyone. All I ask is that you don't complain about my moving. It is not goodbye; it is always see you later.

TTFN,

Brooke Stevens

I hit send, grabbed my MP3 player and speakers, and headed in to take a nice relaxing bubble bath. As the tub filled with hot water and bubbles, I went in and poured a glass of wine. After everything I went through the last few days, I thought it was well deserved. I returned to the bathroom, pressed play so I could listen to my favorite playlist, and then relaxed in the nice hot water. I could hear my phone ringing in the other room, and decided I would just call whoever it was back later. Nothing was going to disturb my relaxation. An hour later I finished my glass of wine I had been nursing, decided I looked enough like a prune, and it was time to get out. I dried off, put on my nice comfy robe and headed to check my phone for messages. One missed call from an unknown number and no message. "I guess it wasn't that important," I thought to myself out loud. I got dressed and started to plan dinner. Dad was running low on food, so eating out sounded like a great idea. I sat in dad's recliner and watched another show on the DVR while I waited for him to get home from work. By the time he got home I had drifted off to sleep.

"Was it that hard of a day?" He asked after waking me up. "I guess you decided not to cook. I can make us some cans of soup if you would like."

"No I…." I was cut off by the ringing of my phone.

"Hello?"

"Hello Brooke this is Diana. I showed you some houses earlier."

"I remember. Do you have an answer already? That was extremely fast."

"I do have an answer for you. They rejected your offer. They did however come back with a counter offer. After they heard who you were, they said they couldn't have you pay that much. They were asking double what the house is worth in this town. They knew if someone was willing to pay double, they must really love and want the house. So the good news is that their counter offer is $200,000. What do you think?"

"OMG! That's amazing. I'll take it. When can I come in and sign the papers?"

"I'll have them drawn up by noon tomorrow and call you so you have time to go the bank for a cashier's check. Congratulations. Starting tomorrow you will officially be a homeowner. I'll talk to you tomorrow."

"Thank you so much. I will keep my phone next to me awaiting your call." I hung up the phone with the biggest grin on my face.

"Who was that and why are you so happy?"

"Get changed and I'll show you why I am so happy at dinner tonight. Hurry up. I can't wait to show you."

I waited impatiently for Dad to shower and change out of his work clothes. I thought I would wear a hole in the floor pacing back and forth. As soon as he was ready, we headed out to my surprise.

"Why are we going out here? It is the middle of nowhere. Have you lost your damn mind?"

"Just relax Dad. We are almost there, I promise. I really think you will love this surprise." A few minutes later we pulled up in front of the house.

"I have seen this house before. What's so special about it?"

"I put in an offer on it today."

"Why would you do that? They are asking double what it is worth."

"I know, but I fell in love with it. The good news is, they know who I am and rejected my offer. They came back with a counter offer of $200,000. I accepted and will sign the papers tomorrow. It's my house dad. SURPRISE!" I yelled. "As soon as possible I will head to Kansas City, pack my belongings, and officially move back to my hometown. Are you as excited as I am?"

"That is wonderful news. Let's go celebrate with dinner at Sweet & Salty Eats."

"Let's go eat and talk plans. I love you Dad. I can't wait to be back here full time"

We drove to the diner and sat in the booth we used to call ours when I was a child and I explained my reason for buying that house. "It is such a beautiful place. The outside looks original. In the last year the current owners did some remodeling on the inside. Bedrooms were smaller back in the Civil War era, so they turned two rooms into one and added a master bathroom with a walk-in closet. It's the dream room. They also updated the kitchen so it's perfect for me. I know the house is big for just one person, but maybe someday I'll have a family of my own, or you may decide you can't or don't want to live on your own. There's plenty of room for a family and my wonderful father."

"I was wondering why you chose such a big house. After you find out when you can move in and get things settled in Kansas City, we can go furniture shopping."

"I would like that. For my other surprise I made another huge decision. I know you're working overtime so you can keep up with paying the mortgage. I want to pay it off for you. Please let me do this. You have been working far too hard for far too long. It's time for you to relax a little bit."

"You're already buying a house. I can't let you do that."

"Too late, I already went to the bank and spoke to them about it. Next week it will be a done deal." I stuck out my tongue like a little kid.

"You are the best daughter a father could ask for." he cried.

We finished dinner and headed home. We spent the rest of the night watching movies and chatting before heading to bed. The next day I signed the papers, made arrangements for my move, and made a few calls. I told Chief Parks that I would take the job and told Clara's lawyer that I would like to start the interviews the next day. The rest of the day was filled with sitting around and relaxing.

Chapter Five

On the morning of my first interview with Clara, I woke up with my stomach in knots. For the life of me I could not understand why I agreed to listen to her tell me all the gruesome details of the murders. Was finding out the truth about my mother's murder really worth going through all of this? Could there be an easier way to get the evil monster to fess up to what she knows? I wasn't sure if I could go through with it. I was so far past nervous at this point. I couldn't think of any other way to do this.

"I have to do this." I told myself. "There is no other way. Suck it up and get ready to go. Stop being such a coward." After giving myself a crazy pep talk, I rushed around and got ready. I wanted to pick up another recorder, just in case there were any problems with the one I already had. I also needed more notebooks and pencils. I headed off to get the things needed and go to the police station.

I was greeted by Chief Parks as soon as I entered the building. We spent a few minutes going over the rules.

"Hello Brooke. Are you ready to go over the rules? There aren't many, but they are important."

"I'm ready. I think I can handle this." I paused for a minute. "No, I know I can handle this."

"I'm glad you are willing to help, and I want to say thank you." He smiled at me trying to help calm my nerves. "The first rule is, that you do not hand Clara anything. You also do not accept anything she may try to give you. No matter what she says, you cannot let her see fear in your eyes. Recording devices are not allowed, but we have made an exception for this case. Since she has already admitted to her guilt and you are using this information for more than just to help us, we are allowing it. The last rule is easy. No matter what she says or does, you cannot touch her in anyway. This means no slapping, punching, or hurting her in anyway. She will most likely try and push your buttons. You can't let her do that. As long as you understand everything I will take you into the room."

"I understand. I am very nervous, but I can do this. You don't need to worry so much."

I was taken into the same room as last time. Clara was already in the room waiting and this time there was a different chair. A nice plush office chair that made me smile when I saw it, but it quickly changed to a scowl when I noticed Clara staring at me. Chief Parks exited the room, closing the door behind him. I took my seat, pulled out my first notebook, a recorder, and got everything ready.

"Aren't you going to greet me? I can't be interviewed by someone who is rude. At least pretend you're interested in more than just my secret. If you don't want to do this I'll find someone else," Clara snapped.

"I'm sorry. How are you today Clara? Are they treating you well? Would you like something to drink before we begin?" I tried to act like I cared.

"That's more like it," she smirked. "See you can be nice. It will make this go by faster. If I am allowed I would like some water please."

"Can we please get Clara some water, and I would like a soda. Thank you!" I told the guard, who called out the order on his walkie. A few minutes later Officer Galloway entered with our drinks. He smiled as he handed mine to me and then quickly exited the room. I smiled as I watched him leave.

"Got a crush on 'Pig' Galloway? That's so cute." She smiled making me feel uncomfortable. "Where would you like to start? Should I just jump in and tell you about my victims, or do you want my whole pathetic life story?" she stared at me, and I felt as though I had been violated.

"Why don't you start with why you decided to kill 6 innocent people, or would that make you too sad?" I suggested trying to mess with her head.

"I like your attitude and your style. You remind me of myself when I was younger. I am sure you already know about the abuse my mother thrust upon me by staying with my no good son of a bitch father. Half of the time she just left the room while he was beating me. The other half she was too busy crying like a baby to defend me. I hated her for it. If she had a backbone, I wouldn't even be here. She should have left him before I was even conceived. Because she chose to stay with him, I saw and went through things no child should ever have to deal with. He never sexually abused me, but there was a lot of physical and mental abuse. My mom made me out to be a clumsy child every time she took me to the emergency room." Her look was full of anger I had never seen before.

"I remember when I was 5 years old. I asked him if I could have a Popsicle and he told me to ask my mom. When I told him she wasn't home yet, he said 'Just wait til she gets home and ask her. Like any little kid I threw a temper tantrum. He was so angry that he threw the TV remote at me making me cry louder which only pissed him off more. He told me to stop acting like a whiney fucking brat or he would make me pay. I didn't understand why he was being so mean, so I called him a poopy head. That was a huge mistake. He dragged me across the living room and into the kitchen by my hair. While being dragged I hit my head on the corner of the coffee table, the leg of a chair, and the door frame that lead into the kitchen. When we reached the kitchen he pulled out a wooden handled cutting board. I saw it and started screaming. He responded, 'If you want to scream, I'll give you a reason to.' He then smacked me across the face with the cutting board repeatedly. I know he hit me at least 6 times before I passed out." She looked as though she might cry before turning to a look of irritation. "When I woke up in the hospital the next day, I had a swollen eye along with a swollen cheek and four missing teeth. My mother was sitting next to me crying. The first thing she said to me was the first proof that she didn't care about me at all. 'Clara sweetie, you have to be careful when you play with the neighbors' horse. You know the mule they have is mean.' Not once did she ask if I was okay, or tell me she loved me. That was just the first of many emergency room visits that I remember."

"Do you need me to slow down, or should I continue?" She looked so angry.

"Keep going. I will let you know if I have any questions. I know it doesn't make things better, but I am truly sorry you had to go through that. No child should ever be treated like you were." I tried to show some sympathy as I finally started to understand why she was so twisted.

"I don't want or need your damn sympathy," she spat. "Anyway, I think you get the idea of how my childhood was. I say we get to the fun stuff. Part of the reason you are here." She sounded as if she was half laughing, half howling. "I'm sure you know by now that I am not like all the other serial killers. I do not have an MO, no fetishes, and I do not 'get off' on murdering people. I killed each victim in a different way. The only thing that was the same was that I kept their wallets and purses. I didn't see the point in boring myself with killing everyone the same way. There is no remorse and I loved tossing the bodies or body parts into a nice big hole I dug. I dug the hole for all those damn rocks and boulders, but it just seemed to be too boring of a hole. That's when I decided to spice it up with a few bodies. It was all too easy to get them over to my house. People will believe anything you tell them these days. I just wish I could be out there gathering more stupid people. I was just doing the world a favor. Don't you agree?"

"I'm sorry but I can't agree with you on this. Just because someone is gullible doesn't mean they should be killed." The look of confusion must have made her mad as she stood as much as she could and slammed her fists on the table. This got the guards attention and he yelled for her to sit down or he would use the taser on her.

She sat back in her chair with a look of disgust. "So you think it is ok that we are overrun with stupid people in this world? I guess you are not as smart as I thought you were. Maybe I should find someone smarter to do this interview. Can you at least act smart during the interviews, or are you just a worthless piece of shit?"

"Excuse me? I came here to do you a favor. You said I was the only one you would talk to. If you would rather I just say you are an arrogant, psychotic, no good bitch with daddy issues that can be arranged." I glared at her with determination in my eyes. I had to show her I could play the game too. "What is it going to be Clara? Interview, or I make up whatever I feel like?"

"So you think you can play my game? Let me tell you all about victim number one, or should I say number two."

"Go ahead, but know that nothing you say or do will scare me or get to me in any way." I smiled as I lied through my teeth. The fact was that this scared me more than anything else in my life, but I could not let Clara know that. No matter what she said, I had to be strong, confident, and bluff my way through this. I knew it would work.

"Let's see how weak your stomach truly is. Sharon Russell, what can I say about her? If I remember correctly she was 34 years old. I knew when I saw her that she was new to town. I approached her for the first time at the grocery store. Poor thing looked lost, so I asked if she needed help finding something. She said she was looking for a certain type of brownie. We talked as I showed her where they were located. I grabbed a few things so I didn't look suspicious and helped her find the rest of the food on her list. We checked out and I went to my car. As I was driving home I noticed the poor woman walking home. I offered to give her a ride. She thanked me and said she was new in town, and had just moved to Brines for her job. I asked if she wanted to come to my house and hang out for awhile. She said no at first, until I told her she could put the cold groceries in my fridge while she was there. She finally agreed to come over."

"When we got to my house, I helped her bring in the cold groceries and place them in my fridge. I offered her a glass of wine which she quickly accepted. We sat in awkward silence for several minutes before I decided to start a conversation. I told her I loved her long beautiful hair. I said I was jealous and always wanted black hair like hers." Clara grinned as she recalled the memory. "Then we talked about where she was from, Waterloo, Iowa. I told her Iowa stood for Idiots Out Wandering Around and we both laughed. We sat talking and drinking for several hours. What she didn't know is that I wasn't drinking at all. I just made her think I was."

"How did you make her think you were drinking?" I said confused.

"I poured her wine, until she drank almost two bottles. I

said I was drinking vodka, but it was just water and was very easy to fake. After a few hours she was plastered, so I offered for her to stay the night. I told her I had a finished basement. It was fully furnished, like it was a little apartment. She agreed thinking I was too drunk to drive her home. I helped her down the basement stairs and I led her to my 'special' room. When she saw the room she freaked out. I pushed her into the room and closed the door behind us. Poor thing was so drunk she didn't even notice the closed door, and ran right into it. She knocked herself out cold. It was like watching a cartoon and I loved it. Luckily she was very light so I lifted her easily onto the table and strapped her to it. I placed a gag in her mouth for fun. I didn't need to use it due to the room being soundproof." She looked delighted. "Can't have people hearing what I am doing can I? After I made sure she was secure and there was no possible way for her to escape I locked her in the room and went up to sleep."

"The next morning I got up and fixed breakfast. I was in no hurry, and wanted her to be as scared as possible before I started the fun. I thought of ways to kill her. Should I do it quickly or slowly over several days? I settled on slow and painful. I planned it all out and went to the hardware store to buy the final products I would need. I asked for some liquid fire saying I had a slow draining tub. The wonderful young man, unaware he was helping aid me in my first murder, showed me where it was. He warned me it was basically acid and showed me the correct protective gear I would need. Such a sweet and caring young man. That's rare these days you know. I thanked him, paid for the items, and drove home. I was as excited as a kid in a candy store and could not wait to get started."

"You said you don't get off on killing people. Is it the torture that excites you? To me it sounds like torture is better than sex in your mind."

"I was not sexually excited you dumbass," she hissed. "Now where was I? Oh, yes. Day one of torture. You will love this, I promise. It's better than any scene in a movie you have ever seen. It makes me smile just thinking about it. I started her torture nice and easy. I moved the straps around her ankles further up on her legs. I smiled when I saw the panic in her eyes. I decided she wasn't quite freaked out enough, so I went up stairs and got my MP3 player. Gotta have good music to torture people to, am I right? Everything you do needs a playlist. It makes life better. I hooked it up to a speaker, cranked up the sound, covered them with plastic, and started up the wood burning stove. After that the fun began. I told her if she promised not to scream I would remove the gag. With her big brown eyes full of tears she nodded to let me know she would cooperate. I had to toy with her, so I removed the gag and told her if she behaved I would let her go. She cried as she told me she would do anything I asked her to, and she begged me not to hurt her. The poor woman had no idea what was in store for her over the next three days. I still smile. The first kill is always the sweetest."

"How did you 'toy' with Sharon? Is there a reason you have only said her name once? I'm just curious, whether it bothers you, or if you just hate her name," I pried.

She once again laughed sounding almost like a hyena

this time. "Why would Sharon's name bother me? I do hate the name. It made killing her more fun. To answer your first question, I made her promises, and she thought I would let her leave. I did, in the end, let her leave, just not alive. The first thing I did was put a pot of water on top of the wood stove. I told her I was going to make us some noodles with butter and garlic for lunch. I let the water boil, and cooked the noodles. As the noodles were cooking I cut open her shirt, cut the bra off exposing her naked breasts, and ran the knife lightly down from her chest to her belly button. She cried even harder and kept begging me not to kill her. I placed the knife on the counter and then removed some ice from the freezer in the back corner. Then it was time for the real fun to begin. I grabbed a towel so I wouldn't burn myself and picked up the pan of boiling water and noodles. I then proceeded to slowly dump the contents over Sharon's naked chest. As she screamed in pain from the burns, I grabbed the ice and placed the cubes in random places on the burned area causing her skin to dry and crack in some places, and other places quickly developed the biggest blisters I had ever seen in my life. I cried tears of joy as I looked upon my work. I let out a small giggle as I touched the hot pan to the side of her face. I held it there for approximately 10 minutes, before pulling it away with a couple layers of her skin."

"You're truly a sick individual. I just don't understand why you enjoyed this so much." I shook my head in disgust at Clara.

"Hey I don't judge you Miss Goody Two Shoes. We all love different things in life, so just get over thinking you're better than me. Do you want to hear more?"

"Please go on," I replied motioning at her to continue.

"Thank you," she retorted sharply. "I left her like she was for awhile and went up stairs to eat dinner. I took my time so I could drag the torture out longer. After about two hours I had finished eating, washed my dishes, and cleaned up my mess. I went down to the basement to make sure Sharon wasn't dead. It would have ruined everything if she was dead so soon. I had some wonderful plans for her. I was thrilled to see that she was still alive and in severe pain. I decided to have a little more fun before I went to sleep for the night. I grabbed the knife I used earlier to expose her bare skin, and started to slowly cut and pop a few of her bigger blisters. The pain caused her to scream out and eventually pass out. I cleaned the oozing pus that splattered onto my hands and went up stairs locking the door behind me as I left. The next day I went about as if it was business as usual. I ate at the diner, visited my mom in the hospital, read her part of her favorite book, and headed home."

"What happened to your mom to put her in the hospital? Is she sick?" I asked with concern in my voice.

"I will tell you about that another time. After I got home, I watched a movie, texted with a couple of my friends, and prepared for my next round of fun. I relit the wood burning stove, and asked Sharon if she was ready for some fun? She turned her head away from me which pissed me off. I grabbed a leather strap and tied her head tight enough that she couldn't move it. I then checked the fire and determined it was almost hot enough. While I waited for the flames to get bigger I grabbed two belts. One at a time I wrapped and tightened them about three inches above her ankles. I opened the stove again and placed a large, flat metal disk on top of the flames. I then grabbed my chainsaw, and started it up. I saw the look of sheer terror on her face. I smiled and started cutting through her ankles. As the blood splattered, and showered me and the room, I laughed. The more she screamed, and the more blood flying through the air, the happier I was. I had so much fun that I can't even remember how long it took. Once they were removed I grabbed a pair of long tongs used for grilling and removed the hot disk from the fire. I carefully placed it on one leg and then the other to cauterize the wounds. I couldn't have her bleeding to death on me. When I looked at her face, I noticed she had passed out on me again. Her passing out was really making me mad so I gave up and removed my blood drenched clothing and went up to take a shower and go to bed."

"I can see your stomach is churning. Shall I go on? I'm almost done."

"I'm fine, please continue." I lied wanting to be done for the day.

"I'll skip my boring day and go straight to the final moments of fun since it was a normal day for me. A day of acting like everyone else you know. I waited until 10:00 pm to finish Sharon off. When I went back down I was wearing my protective gear and carrying a bottle of Liquid Fire. To my sheer delight Sharon was awake. This time instead of crying and looking afraid, she had a look of pure hatred. As I leaned down to tell her goodbye, she spit in my face. I carefully opened the bottle of liquid fire and poured a small amount on her left knee. She didn't scream or cry so I poured some onto the crotch of her pants. She still did not scream out. So I poured a small amount on her left breast. I stood and watched as it bubbled and ate through her skin. I watched as a hole formed in her chest exposing her still beating heart. It was then that I grabbed the knife and stabbed her, putting an end to her pathetic life. An hour or so later I removed all of the restraints, grabbed a tarp to wrap her in, cleaned up a bit, and dragged her out the basement door and up the stairs to a wheelbarrow. I took her body to the hole I had previously dug, dumped the body, threw some rocks on it, and went back inside to clean up the room. I spent the night cleaning, took a shower, and went to bed."

I turned my head and unable to hold anything in, I threw up all over the floor. Without saying a word, I gathered my belongings and rushed out of the room. I told Uncle David I would call later, but that I needed to go home and try to get the images out of my head. Officer Galloway ran over to me and made sure I was going to be alright. I assured him I was fine and went home. I knew I wasn't going to get any sleep, so I curled up in bed with a book and read.

Stephanie Brown

Chapter Six

The first night after the interview I could not eat or sleep. It was still difficult to eat the next day as the images were still fresh in my mind. It took three days before I could sleep. It was a fitful sleep, but better than nothing. A week after the first interview I went back to the station for the second one. I hoped I could handle this one better than the last. When I was taken into the room, Clara was again waiting for me with a look of joy in her eyes. I hated that telling me about the torture and murder of others made her so happy, but if I was going to find out if she knew anything about my mother, I was going to have to keep doing this. "Be strong," I told myself. I faked a smile, nodded and prepared for another day of pure torture. "Shall we begin?" I asked.

"I would love to start. Maybe this time you can handle it."

"I know you get a kick out of this, but I don't. Not everyone is a neurotic, crazy psychopathic freak. Just get on with it already," I responded.

"Sounds like someone is in a bad mood, so I will begin with victim number two today. On June 8th I met Randy Dugan at the bar downtown. He told me he was 37 and in town for a family float trip. He was very tall. I would say about six foot, with short messy blond hair, and the oddest blue eyes. In fact one eye was larger than the other. He was an overweight man, so I knew he would be an easy target. We spent a couple of hours drinking. I of course had soda instead of alcohol. I flirted, even though I was not even remotely interested, so when I asked him if he wanted to get out of there and have some fun he agreed. I explained to him that my house was the better option, because I was a screamer. I really do swear that he was more excited by hearing that than anything else I said that night. So I drove us over to my house. The poor man had no idea what he was in for."

"Did he at least get any action before you killed him?" I laughed. It was one of the few things I really wanted to know.

"That's a good question and no he did not. Shortly after we got to my place I asked him to get me a bottle of wine from the basement. I showed him where the basement door was, and as he started down the stairs, I pushed him. Unfortunately for me, it didn't knock him out. I pretended it was an accident due to a dizzy spell. He asked if I was okay, and I told him I was. As I descended the stairs he stood up. I asked him if he liked things a little rough. The excitement on his face told me he did. I took his hand and showed him into my room. Since I had already decided my next target would be male, I had redesigned the room a bit to look like it was a sex chamber. We walked in and I locked the door behind us."

"So you bought sex toys that you had no intention of using? That's very strange to me," I laughed.

"Of all the things I have said, that's what intrigues you most?" She returned the laugh.

I looked her in the eyes. "That stuff isn't cheap. You should at least use it once if you are going to buy it."

"Good point. Too late now. They won't let me have that

stuff in prison, nor will they let any men near me. Back to what happened. He asked if I wanted to be tied up, and I told him I was always the dominant one. He groaned and said I was killing him. He had no idea. He stripped naked and hopped up on the table, laid down, and told me to be as rough as I wanted. While I strapped him to the table I told him the safe word was 'igloo.' I actually had to stop myself from puking. He just might be the most disgusting man in the entire world. I placed a ball gag in his mouth, tightened it, and went over to get my 'toys.' I started by grabbing a cat 'o nine tails. I had a little bit of fun beating the hell out of him. After a few minutes he caved and started yelling the safe word. So I played along and stopped. I went over to a drawer and pulled out a blindfold, and placed it over his eyes. I explained to him that I wanted the next toy to be a surprise. That gave the pervert an instant hard on. I went back to the drawer and pulled out a filleting knife." Clara half smiled at me.

"OMG! Did you castrate him?" I exclaimed.

"No, that would have been too nice for him, so I just injured him a bit. I started with the left nipple and sliced it right off. He tried to scream, but I shoved the ball gag further into his mouth. I ran the blade lightly down his body to his balls. I carefully sliced off the top layer of skin. It was so much fun watching him squirm. I removed skin in a few more places, loosened the gag, and went up stairs to sleep."

"The next morning, while eating breakfast I decided he was too much of a pig to let live much longer. I cleaned up, grabbed the salt, and went back to work on him. I searched the drawer for a pair of tweezers. He still had the blindfold on, so he had no idea what was next. I very slowly pulled off all of his finger nails and toe nails. After that, I poured salt on all of his wounds. I quickly got bored and decided to research how to do what I planned to do next. After a few hours, I determined that I would place a trash can next to the table and drain him of his blood slowly. I grabbed my knife, some thin rubber tubing, and got to work. I carefully put a small slit in his wrist, inserted the tubing into his vein, and let it all drain out over time into the trash can. The next morning, I did chest compressions on him to make sure he was empty. When the blood stopped dripping from his body, I removed the gag and blindfold. I got out my chainsaw and cut him into smaller easier to carry pieces. I waited until midnight when I knew it was safe, carried him piece by piece to the wheelbarrow, and dumped him into the hole with more rocks."

"Didn't take you long to kill Randy. We still have time if you want to start telling me about the third victim," I suggested. Even if I didn't want to hear anymore, I knew the more I heard in a day, the faster it would be over with.

"I would love to keep telling you about my accomplishments. Number three was Billy McGowan. I met him on June 27th while he was taking pictures downtown. I struck up a conversation with him and was able to find out that he was living his dream of traveling the country and taking pictures of small towns. He showed me some of the photos he had taken of Brines. Billy took the most amazing pictures I have ever seen. I was almost sad that he was going to be next. He was tall, about 43, with short salt and pepper hair, and sexy brown eyes. We talked about life, following our dreams, and the things we loved most about small towns. I explained that I lived in small towns my whole life and loved how close and friendly everyone was. He told me that he spent most of his life in big cities and was currently living in Brentwood, California. It wasn't as large as Chicago or New York and had approximately 55,000 people. He also told me he was thinking about moving to a small town soon. After talking for a couple of hours, we said our goodbyes and I headed to my car. I stood next to it for a few minutes before walking back over to where he was taking more pictures. As I walked towards him I started to cry and pretend I was upset. When he asked what was wrong I indicated that I had locked my keys in my car. I also told him that I couldn't afford to pay for someone to unlock it for me and asked if he would give me a ride to my house so I could get my spare keys. He hesitated, so I shrugged and started walking home. After walking for a good fifteen minutes, his car pulled up next to me. Billy apologized for being so rude and agreed to take me to get my keys. On the drive to my house the only words spoken were directions on how to get there. When we arrived, I asked if he would like to come in and wait while I found the keys. He declined saying he was going to wait outside so he could smoke a cigarette. I giggled a bit and let him know he could smoke in my house and the only reason I didn't have one lit was because they were locked in my car. He agreed to come in and offered me a smoke. As he sat on the couch smoking, I pretended to search for my keys and continued to talk with him."

"I'm surprised you killed him," I smirked. "It sounds like the two of you had a connection of some kind. As if an invisible force drew the two of you together. Was he easy to kill?"

"He was the most difficult of all my victims. I thought about just having sex with him and letting him go, but my passion for my 'art,' as I call it, was a stronger feeling deep inside of me. Besides, all men want is sex and to control you. I was not going to be weak like my mother. No man was ever going to use, control, or beat me. I was in charge of my own life." She had a confident look upon her face.

"Not all men are like your father. My father isn't like that. He's loving, and caring. He treats me with respect. Well 90% of the time he does, the other 10% he's still acting like I'm a fragile little girl who needs protecting. He tried his hardest to keep me from speaking to you, but eventually caved when he realized I was old enough and strong enough to take care of myself. He knew I could handle it. That's how most men behave. I only got my ass beat once, and to be honest, if I had a child who did what I had done, I would beat their ass just the same."

"Well good for you on being one of the few who had a good father. Not all of us are so lucky you know." Clara looked at me once again full of anger and hatred.

"I am so sorry," I replied knowing she killed so many innocent people, but understanding her motives a little more. I really did feel sorry for her, even though I tried my damndest not to. "Please continue."

"It's okay, I like having conversations with you. You may not agree with what I did, but at least, for the most part, you try to be understanding of my past." For the first time she had a sincere smile on her face. "I told Billy I remembered where my spare keys were and that I needed to go to the basement to get them. He smiled and watched me as I walked out of the room. I acted like the door was stuck, when I realized he had followed me down the stairs. I looked over at him with an innocent look on my face and asked if he could please help me open the door. I led him to believe that it was my old bedroom, and I must have left the keys in there. He smiled and walked to the door. While he had his back turned to me, I grabbed a baseball bat leaning against a box and as he easily opened the door, I hit him as hard as I could. His body dropped to the floor with a loud thump. I struggled for about an hour to get him up and into a thick metal chair that was bolted to the floor on the other side of the room. I strapped him to it very tight. He was much harder to maneuver than I thought he would be. I found his car keys in his pocket, and drove his car into the barn to keep it hidden."

"How did you get your car back? Did you have to walk to town to get it?" I inquired.

"I'll get to that in a few." She was clearly irritated by my interruption. "I went back down to make sure the blow to the head hadn't killed him. He was very much alive, but still unconscious. I decided it was safe to leave him alone and locked him up tight in the room. I headed over to my neighbor Echo's house to ask her for a ride to get my car. She looked confused so I had to make up a lie. I said a friend brought me home so we could have a little fun. We fooled around a bit, I passed out, and when I woke up he was gone. She gladly took me to get my car and we parted ways. I stopped at Sweet & Salty Eats to get a quick bite to eat, and decide just how I wanted to torment Billy. The more pain I could cause the better, but I needed something new. I returned home and decided to watch a few movies to try and get some new inspiration. Billy wasn't going anywhere, so I figured I had plenty of time to do my research. None of the films I watched were even remotely helpful, so I chose to just wing it. I would do whatever came to my mind at the time."

"Sorry, but I thought serial killers planned out their murders in advance. I know you did things differently, but shouldn't you have planned a little more?" I challenged.

"I suppose I should have planned everything in advance, but to be totally honest, I didn't know I would enjoy it so much. I thought my first victim would be the only one. I left Billy down there alone for the first night. I wanted to be well rested and clear headed for what I was going to do. I knew I was in for some fun times. When I awoke, I started my day as normal, before heading down to see Billy. When I opened the door I could hear his screaming. He asked me to let him go and promised he wouldn't tell anyone. He begged and pleaded for about an hour and tried to convince me he would leave town immediately and never speak a word of what had happened the night before. I laughed and told him it was cute that he had the idea I would let him go. He wouldn't stop begging, even after I yelled at him to shut up, and smacked him across the face. I ran up stairs and grabbed a couple of muscle relaxers from the medicine cabinet, crushed them up, and put them in some orange juice. It took some convincing but after about an hour he agreed to drink it."

"How did you convince him to do that?" I looked surprised.

She had a sickeningly sweet look on her face that sent shivers down my spine. "I told Billy I needed him to drink it so he could keep up his strength. When he asked why, I told him I could not have sex with a man who was too weak to get it up. I guess he thought that maybe I was just into kink, we would have sex, and I would let him go home. Boy was he wrong. I put the straw in his mouth and he drank it down faster than I have ever seen anyone drink in my life. See, I told you men were pigs. I told him to relax and try to get in the mood while I went to change into something sexier."

"Did you change into something sexy?" I pried.

"No I didn't. Instead I stayed upstairs and played a game on my computer. I needed to give the meds time to work. Before you ask about how many pills I gave him. One pill always made me pass out so I knew two would work on a man of his height and size. After about an hour I grabbed my grandma's old sewing box and prepared for my first task. As I suspected he was passed out cold and it made my job so much easier. I threaded the needle with the toughest thread I could find and began sewing his mouth shut. I started by holding the inside of his lips closed with some Gorilla Glue. Once I knew it was dry enough to hold his mouth closed, I inserted the needle into the bottom of his lower lip, and up through his top lip. I made the stitches as tight as I could and very close together. No more screaming or talking from him. It would be a wonderful surprise when he woke up. I was tired from everything I had done lately so I grabbed a blanket and pillow from the couch and went back down stairs to nap in my beautiful room. I wanted to be there when he woke up and realized he could no longer speak."

"Wasn't that uncomfortable? How did you sleep on such a hard surface?" I was puzzled as to how anyone could handle it for more than a few minutes.

She had a sad look on her face. "When I was little I didn't have a bed. I was forced to sleep on the floor. If I was a good little girl," she cried, "I was allowed a pillow and blanket. Only good children got spoiled. My father was such a generous man, don't you think?" Clara ridiculed.

"Sounds like a total sweetheart," I joked trying not to make light of her situation.

"Tell me about it," she laughed. "Anyway, the medicine knocked him out longer than I thought it would. I slept the rest of the afternoon and all night long. In fact I was up before him. I panicked thinking he may be dead. I had so many more things I wanted to do to him. Thankfully he was still alive and kicking, so to speak. I determined that a little torture would wake him right up. It took me a few minutes to think of what would be the best thing to do. I squealed with delight when the idea hit me. I raced up to my bathroom and grabbed my curling iron. I was so full of excitement as I descended the stairs. I entered the room and went to the nearest wall plug, and plugged it in to start the heating process. It was going to be so much fun waking Billy up. I turned on my music and danced around the room while I waited. As I checked the warmth of the curling iron and determined it was hot enough, my favorite song came on. I danced over to Billy's body and placed the hot curling iron against his left eye. As I suspected it woke him right up. He tried to open his mouth to scream, but due to the glue and my handy stitching, he was unable to and caused himself more pain. After a few minutes, I switched to his right eye. He couldn't see it, but I had the biggest smile on my face. It was the most fun I had ever had and I loved the smell of his burning flesh. As I removed the curling iron I leaned over and whispered in his ear. 'Do you still love it here in the small town of Brines?' He shook his head no which made me giggle more. I then taped gauze taut over his eyes to make sure he didn't bleed to death. I still had more plans in store for him."

"Would you like to take a break to eat?" I Asked. Surprisingly I was hungry and thought I might be able to eat.

"That's a great idea. I will see you after we eat. That's when the real fun will begin." She nodded towards the guard.

I turned off the recorder, and packed up to go eat. When I got to the diner, I was met by my dad and a couple of his friends from work.

"Hey Dad. How are you doing today?"

"Brooke, are you done with your work for the day? I thought it would take a lot longer. She didn't upset you too much did she?" he sounded so concerned.

"We just decided to take a break to eat, that's all. Can we talk about something else please? I need happy things to discuss," I begged.

"I think that's a good idea. You remember Ethan and Frank from work don't you? Of course you do, how could you forget these two weirdos." He shook his head. "I was telling them about you quitting your job, buying a house here in Brines, paying off my mortgage, and the new temporary job at the police station. I am just so proud of you lately. Despite interviewing a dangerous serial killer, you are trying to do what you love in a different way. You've always loved to write, and now you can do it on your own terms."

"Aww Daddy. Thank you for being so supportive. Hello Ethan and Frank, how has everything been going since I saw you last? I see you still work at the factory. Either of you planning on retiring any time soon?" I smiled.

Ethan acted as though it had been 20 years since he last saw me. "Let's see, you've been gone for what 30 years or so now?" We all burst into laughter. "It's so good to see you again. I'm still at the factory, still married to my beautiful wife of 28 years, and the kids are doing great, except for little Sara."

"What's wrong with Sara? Is she okay? Why didn't anyone call me?" I exclaimed.

"I thought your dad told you. Last year Sara was heading to the mall with her favorite Uncle Frank." He looked at Frank with a reassuring smile. "A car ran through a stop sign and hit them. The car rolled four times. Sara and Frank were crushed in the car. Because Sara was so little the impact of the airbag knocked her unconscious, and pieces of the steering wheel ended up embedded in Frank's neck. Sara went through several surgeries and spent three months in a coma. Frank also underwent major surgery. He died on the table twice. Sara ended up with brain damage and Frank is no longer able to speak. I get to come to dinner with the guys once a month and I told my wife she needs to go out once a week. She stays at home taking care of Sara every day, so she needs it. I keep telling Frank it's not his fault, but you know how he is. He's a great man, and nothing will change that."

"I'm so very sorry. Sara is such a sweet little girl. I guess I missed a lot being gone so long. I'll have to stop by and visit when I have time. Frank, you know he's right. None of this is your fault." I squeezed his hand.

I looked at the time on my phone and realized I needed to get back to the interview. I finished my food, got a refill of my soda in a to go cup, paid my bill, and said good bye to the guys.

When I returned to the station and I entered the room before Clara. I got everything set back up and quietly waited for her return. Fifteen minutes later she was led into the room, and secured to the floor.

"Welcome back Clara. Did you enjoy your meal?"

She shrugged, "It was okay I guess. They need to learn how to use spices. It's so bland. Now where were we?"

"You just bandaged Billy's eyes to make sure he wouldn't bleed to death. I'm assuming you spent the rest of the day doing normal people things?" I asked.

"Normal people things? Do you mean eat, clean house, work, and what not?" she stared at me confused.

"That's what I mean. Anything that doesn't have to do with the torture and murder of others is all I meant by it," I assured her.

"Yes, I left the house and went to work. It wasn't a real job per se, but I helped a friend with her goat farm. She can't drive a manual transmission so I help her once a week. When I got home I was so tired I skipped dinner and went to sleep. In the morning I went down to check on Billy Boy. I asked if he was awake and he nodded. I toyed with him a bit before heading out to the barn. I wanted to see if Grandma's old pruning shears were still around. Unfortunately they were beyond rusted, so I went to the store and bought a new pair and went to McDonalds for breakfast. As I sat and ate my sandwich, I thought of a better way to remove the bodies from my house. I'm not that big or too strong and that makes it more difficult. My next stop was the hardware store where I got several boards and some nails and discussed with an employee how to build a ramp. When I was satisfied I could build it on my own, I headed home and started building right away."

"Was it difficult to build?" I was extremely curious.

"I am normally really good with tools and building a variety of different things, but it was harder than I thought it would be," she admitted. "It took me about four and a half hours to finish. I peeked in on Billy and found him trying to get loose. I quietly closed the door, went up to have a glass of wine, and get into the killing mood. Not that I needed a push or anything. I finished my glass of pinot and got ready to work. With pruning shears in hand I descended the stairs and entered the room closing the door behind me. I put a tarp on the floor to keep the mess to a minimum and I leaned in and softly whispered in his ear, 'I want to make up for all the pain. How about a nice blow job to make up for how evil I've been?' He shook his head no and I could almost smell his fear. I got down on my knees, unbuttoned his jeans, and he started doing everything possible to get away. I ignored his struggling and continued to open his zipper. I could hear him whimper through his closed mouth and surprisingly he had tears flowing down his cheeks. I used the pruning shears to cut his jeans open some more and reveal his boxers. I then ripped open his boxers and for show let out an excited moan. I lifted up his penis and pulled up on his balls. Holding them in one hand I used the other hand to slowly place the pruning shears around the underneath of his family jewels. This is the only time I ever came close to getting off. As slowly as I could I squeezed the handle, making a nice clean cut. With that he ripped open the stitches on his mouth, and screamed louder than I have ever heard anyone scream in my life. I placed his penis and family jewels in his shirt pocket, tossed the shears on the table, and went up stairs to relax in a nice bubble bath while I waited for him to bleed out."

"Jesus Christ!" I shrieked. "I'm not even a man and that sends pain through my body. I now know how much you truly hate men. Damn it Clara, that was harsh."

"It's not like he needed it anymore. Seriously, what does a dead man need them for? Don't be so sensitive," she chastised.

"I just think that maybe you could have killed him another way, that's all," I clarified.

"Let me finish. After my bath, when I checked on him, he was still alive, and the bleeding had stopped. I had to think of another way to kill him. I sat on the table staring at him for over an hour, when it hit me. I went over to my secret compartment and grabbed my teal Glock 42. I placed it against his left temple, and pulled the trigger. I stared at his lifeless body until around 1:00am, before removing the straps and bringing in the wheelbarrow. I fought with his heavy body, and maneuvered him into it. It was finally time to test out my new ramp. It was easier to get him out of the house, but still not as easy as I wanted it to be. I did however manage to get him to the hole with the others. I cleaned up the room, took a shower, and went to bed."

"I think that's enough for today. Thank you for sharing everything so far." I tried to fake a smile. "I won't be able to return for about a week. I have some things to do out of town. I will call your lawyer to set up the next interview."

"I hope you enjoyed today's retellings of my 'work' as much as I did. I will see you next time." She nodded toward the guard and was uncuffed from the floor and table.

As she was removed from the room, I gathered my belongings and went out to see Uncle David. I gave him an update and told him I would spend a couple of days typing the information I had so far and make copies of the recordings for the case files. I also explained that I needed to go get my stuff moved out of the apartment and spend a couple of days with my friends up in Kansas City. He thought it would be good for me to get away for a while and told me to drive carefully. I left and headed back to my dad's house.

Dad was waiting for me at the house and greeted me with a hug. "How did things go today? Did you learn anything about how her messed up mind works?"

"It went well and I learned that Clara really hates men. I don't want to talk about it though. There's no need for you to be subjected to the horrors I learned today. I really just want to take a nice relaxing bubble bath and go to bed. Today has been a very long and stressful day. Thank you for being here when I got home. I know you had your weekly poker game tonight. Is there still time for you to go?" I asked hoping he could still go.

"Yes Sweetie. I'm heading out now that I know you're home safe. Enjoy your bubble bath and I will see you in the morning." He kissed my forehead and left for his game.

After my bath, I curled up in bed once again and turned on the TV. I watched "Labyrinth" to get my mind off of the day's interview. While I watched the movie I loaded up my laptop and checked to see what emails I had waiting for me. The first was from my ex boss who was still trying to get me to come back to work for him. I sent a short response explaining that I was moving back home to Brines, had bought a house, and found a new job where I could work whatever hours I wanted. I responded to a few emails from friends then shut down my computer and fell asleep.

Chapter Seven

For the next two days I listened to the recordings and typed them out. Hearing Clara explain the gruesome torture and murders of three of her victims was hard enough the first time, but listening to her explain her horrific childhood made me cry. I still couldn't understand how any parent could treat their child so horribly. It was apparent to me that she was full of anger, hatred, and fear of love. I didn't need to be a psychologist to see how hurt she truly was deep down inside. I wanted so much to be able to change her past. Fix things so she wouldn't do all the dreadful things she had done. Although she didn't seem to show any remorse, I clung to the notion that hidden deep down inside of her she did. I couldn't keep this up without telling myself that she didn't really want to hurt those people. She had a good person hiding inside that cold uncaring exterior.

After I printed the files and copied the voice recordings, I went down to the police station to meet with Chief Parks. He was busy so I poured a cup of coffee, grabbed the file, and borrowed an officer's desk. I started reading the reports and trying to not look at the pictures. I was curious to see what others had to say about Clara. Did they know anything about her past? Were there any early signs that she was headed in this direction? As I drank my coffee and pondered the many questions I had, I heard someone clear their throat trying to get my attention.

"Do you always steal people's seats when they leave to make copies?" he looked at me and smiled.

I looked up to see the grin on Officer Galloway's face. "Oh, I'm sorry is this your desk? I didn't think anyone used it since it's almost empty. I just figured they finally got me a desk. You can have it back later. I mean, if you actually do any work around here."

His look turned from happy to see me and teasing to puzzled and confused. "What do you mean by that? I work my ass off. Go use someone else's desk."

Seeing that I dented his ego I leaned back in the chair, looked at his ass and joked, "Doesn't look like you lost your ass at all. It looks good to me."

With a surprised look on his face he broke out into laughter. "So you like my ass huh?"

"Why yes I do." I tried to keep myself from blushing, but it didn't work. "If you sit too much you'll flatten the poor thing. So how often do you go to the gym?"

He pretended to drop his pen and bent down to pick it up almost shoving his ass in my face. Without thinking I reached out and smacked him on the ass. He quickly stood up with the most embarrassed look on his face. The room became silent as everyone stared to see how Officer Galloway would react. When he didn't say anything I swiftly got up and rushed into the bathroom. "I can't believe I just did that," I cried out to myself. After a few minutes, one of the female officers walked in and looked at me with a big grin on her face.

"Why are you hiding in here? You did what all of the women here wish we could. Besides, I think he liked it almost as much as he likes you," she tried to explain.

"He likes me? What gave you that idea? He doesn't

even know me." At this point I thought everyone was playing a prank on me.

"We all see the way he looks at you. When you're around he can barely form a complete sentence. I've watched him stare at you several times. He refuses to leave the station for anything while you are doing your interviews and he won't even sit at his desk. He stands outside the door the entire time with one hand on his gun ready to spring to action at the first sign of danger. He may not know you very well, but he already likes you more than just a friend. Now get out there, smack him on the ass again for all the female officers, and ask him out to dinner. That's an order."

"Okay, okay, I will be out in a minute. I promise." With a nod of her head she left me to figure out my next step. As I stood at the sink staring at myself in the mirror, I realized she was right, and I'm not getting any younger. I quickly walked out of the bathroom, found Officer Galloway, grabbed him by the front of his shirt, pulled him towards me, and started kissing him. When I was done I slapped him on the ass, walked over to grab the files, and told him to pick me up at 6:00 pm for dinner. I promptly walked into Chief Parks office, closed the door behind me, and left Officer Galloway speechless. Through the closed door we could hear the other officers clapping and shouting.

"Impressive Brooke. I had no idea you and Officer Galloway were an item," he laughed.

Feeling myself blushing again I tried to respond, "Well sir, we aren't an item. At least not right now, but he's hot so I decided if he doesn't have the courage to ask me out I'd ask him. I'm sorry for disrupting the station. It won't happen again."

"No need to apologize. We all needed to see that there's still good in this world. Also, don't lie to me. We both know it will happen again. Now down to business so you have time to do your girly stuff before your date tonight." He let out another deep laugh.

Choosing to ignore his last comment I handed him the files along with my work so far. "I typed up the interviews so far and made copies of the voice recordings like I promised. I have the originals, so these can stay in the file."

"You're doing a great job Brooke. I didn't expect any of this until after your final interview. We could use someone like you around here more often. Maybe you should teach a class on how to keep up with your paperwork for my officers."

"Thank you Chief Parks. I just wanted to get this in the file as quickly as possible. I thought it might help the case if you knew more about what she did and what made her so messed up."

"Please call me Jackson. Only the officers are required to call me Chief. How are you doing with the interviews? Are you sure you can keep doing them?" he had concern in his voice.

"I can do this, and I need to do it," I replied. "Sir I'm positive she has information about my mom. I need to know what happened and I'll do this as long as I have to. I do need to take a week or two off though. I want to spend some time with my friends in Kansas City. Plus I need to pack and get all of my stuff moved down here. I already told Clara and talked to her lawyer. They don't mind waiting so I can be here in Brines full time. I want to get moved so I can spend all of my time concentrating on this case. I want to help in any way I can."

"It will be great to have you in town. Now go home and get ready for that hot date tonight. I'll make sure Officer Galloway is off work in time to pick you up. Call me when you get back to town so I know you made it back safely. Enjoy your time off." He motioned for me to go.

I left the office and walked over to Officer Galloway's desk and wrote down my cell number and address. "Don't be late!" I exclaimed as I walked out the door smiling. On the drive home it finally sunk in that I kissed a man I barely knew and ordered him to take me out on a date. "I have lost my damn mind. He's going to think I'm nuts," I uttered to myself. I had never done anything like that before and was shocked beyond words. What was happening to me? I was not the person to take charge of any situation. Was Clara having some kind of effect on me that I didn't realize? I shrugged and continued the drive home quietly contemplating my previous actions.

When I arrived home dad was there. I wasn't expecting him home for a couple more hours. I ran in to make sure he was okay and found him napping on the couch. I quietly closed the door trying to keep from waking him, but my attempt failed as the breeze going through the house slammed the door shut. Dad jumped up and looked as though he were ready to fight off any intruders.

"Whoa Dad. Calm down. It's just me and I'm sorry I woke you," I panicked.

"Thank God. I've had a bad day and I'm not sure I could have fought anyone off. Did you have a good day?" he asked.

"I'll tell you about it in a bit. What happened today? Are you sick? Did you get hurt?" It felt like a game of 20 questions.

"There was a small fire at the factory. Only one injury and it's just a minor burn," he calmly explained.

I rushed over to him and threw my arms around his neck. "You got burned? Are you sure you're going to be fine? Did you go to the hospital?" I questioned.

He hugged me back. "No sweetie. I didn't get burned. Ethan has a small burn on his right hand. It's nothing major. I'll be out of work for a couple of weeks while they try to determine what caused the fire and get everything repaired and up to code. If you would like I can go to Kansas City with you."

"I would love that. My friends have always wanted to meet this perfect dad I told them about. First I need to tell you what happened today, or rather what I did. I have never been so embarrassed in my entire life. I went to the station to turn in my files and let the Chief know I would be gone for a week or two. While I was waiting to talk to him I sat at a desk no one was using at the time. Turns out it was Officer Galloway's desk. We exchanged a few words, I told him he had a nice ass, and he pretended to drop a pen so he could bend over in front of me. So I smacked him on the ass," I admitted.

"You smacked him on the ass? What were you thinking? What did he do?" It was his turn to play 20 questions.

"Well when he didn't say anything I ran to the bathroom embarrassed. A female officer came in and talked to me. She said he liked me and basically told me to get over myself and smack him on the ass again for all the female officers who were not allowed to do so."

"Well did you listen to her?"

"Not completely. I walked up to him, pulled him to me, and kissed him before slapping his ass again and telling him to pick me up at six. So I guess I have a date to get ready for. He's going to think I am nuts and not show up. I just know it."

"He'd be crazy to do that. I'll let you in on a little secret about men. Just don't tell them I told you. We secretly like it when women take charge like that. Now go get ready. I'll eat a TV dinner tonight so you won't have to worry about me."

"Thanks Daddy. I'll see you after awhile," I said as I nervously headed to my room to get ready. I took a quick shower and shaved. You know, just in case. Then I turned on some music and danced around my room as I tried to figure out what to wear. I didn't have very many dress clothes since going out rarely happened, so I settled for my little black dress and laid it nicely on my bed. I headed back into the bathroom to do my hair. I decided to go with a nice high ponytail with a few ringlets hanging down. "I am not wearing make-up," I thought out loud. I looked at the clock and realized I spent too much time finding the perfect dress, so I rushed around and finished getting ready.

As I walked out of my room, the doorbell rang. Unfortunately Dad got there before me.

"Hello Mr. Galloway," my dad said reaching out to shake his hand.

"Please call me Logan," he said shaking Dad's hand. "It is a pleasure to meet you. Officer James talks about you a lot. I promise I won't keep Brooke out all night and I will be a perfect gentleman."

I pushed in between them, took Logan's hand, and rushed him out the door. "Don't wait up dad. I'll be home late. I promise that I won't behave."

Logan opened the car door for me, and yet again I felt my face begin to blush. I felt like a giddy school girl who finally got the nerve to talk to her crush. Neither of us talked for most of the drive to the restaurant. I was too nervous to talk and was feeling sick to my stomach. I hadn't been on a date for four years. I kept thinking of all the things that could go wrong when he finally broke the silence.

"You look beautiful tonight."

"Thank you. You clean up pretty well yourself Logan."

"I hope you like the place we are going for dinner. I was going to take you to the diner, but figured it wasn't nice enough for a first date." His voice was a little shaky which made me feel a little better.

"I'm sure I'll love it. Where are we going and what kind of food do they have?" I asked trying to make conversation.

"It's a surprise. We'll be there in a few minutes."

We sat in silence the rest of the ride. We pulled up to a place I had never been to before. It looked as though it was the first building in a mostly empty area. Though it did look like other buildings were about to go up. I was so scared that I didn't even notice the name of the restaurant when we entered. It was obvious when I looked around that it was a new Japanese style restaurant. "How did he know about my love for sushi?" I thought to myself.

"I hope sushi is okay. Detective James said it was one of your favorites." He smiled as we were taken to our seats. "I called ahead and placed our order, but feel free to order anything you want."

"It's perfect. I guess I've been gone too long. I didn't know there were any Japanese Sushi places around. Thank you so much for bringing me here. I was starting to have withdrawals. Once a month, the newspaper would pay for us to go out to dinner for a business meeting. I thought I'd have to drive two hours to Springfield for sushi. This is so awesome."

As the waitress brought us our drinks we sat staring at each other. Neither of us was sure where to start the conversation and part of me wanted to make out like a silly high school girl. I knew I was going to have to be the one to break the ice this time.

"So Mr. Galloway, how long have you lived and worked in Brines?"

"I've been there for about two years now. I moved to Brines thinking my days would be filled with traffic tickets, the occasional drunk driver, and domestic violence calls. Who knew it would get so exciting in such a small town? How long did you live in Kansas City?"

"I moved to the city about four and half years ago when I got out of a two year journalism school. I found a job at the newspaper and thought it would be my dream job. Little did I know it would take over my whole life and slowly suck out my soul. I also wrote a lot of freelance articles for many big time magazines. I never had time to go out, so I saved up all my money."

"Sounds like an interesting, yet boring, life. I couldn't handle doing nothing but work all of the time. So when are you moving back down here?"

"I'm leaving in a couple of days to spend time with my friends, pack, and move back down here. I never realized just how much I missed my hometown. It will be so nice to be close to my dad again."

"Are you moving in with your dad or getting your own place," he grinned curiously.

"I will not be living with my dad. I bought a house that I fell in love with."

"Which house? There are several I thought about buying before settling for a tiny apartment. The house I wanted was too far out of my price limit at the time."

"I got the old plantation style house out on Bridge Road. They were asking double what it is worth until they found out I was the one interested. I got it for half of their asking price. I can move in about a week from now."

Logan laughed, "That's the house I wanted. I tried for three weeks to get the owners to come down on the price. They just wouldn't do it. Do you know the owners or something?"

"I don't know them, but my dad does. When there was a bad storm about seventeen years ago, he helped fix their roof. They couldn't afford to have it fixed and insurance was refusing to pay. My dad heard about it, gathered a bunch of his friends from town, and they all went over to repair the house for free. Leave it to my dad to do whatever possible to help others. He's such a great man. Anyway they saw my name, remembered me running around in the yard with the other kids, and decided to lower the price. It's stunning on the inside. Maybe you'll get to see it someday," I winked at him.

"Maybe," he winked back. "Do you want to go have a drink after this? I know a bar that has great drinks, and a dance floor."

"That sounds like a great idea."

"Hurry up and eat so we can go dancing then."

We finished our dinner and headed out to the bar. On the drive there he reached over and grabbed my hand. It made my heart skip a beat. At that moment I knew I could easily fall in love with him. We made it to the bar and spent several hours drinking, laughing, and dancing. I was having so much fun when two very drunk men started fighting. Before Logan had a chance to stop the fight, one of the men threw a punch, missed his target, and his fist met my nose knocking me straight to the floor. Logan rushed to check on me and help me up, while the bartender jumped over the bar, bat in hand, and ran the men off. I tried to tell Logan I was fine, but the swelling was getting worse and the bleeding was bad so he picked me up and rushed me to his car. We went straight for the nearest hospital. While he paced the waiting room, he called my father and explained what happened and where we were. When I got out of x-ray both my father and Logan were waiting in my room.

"I'm fine Dad. I promise. You didn't have to rush down here," I tried to convince him.

"You're not fine. Stop trying to act so strong all of the time. It's okay to be 'weak' every once in awhile. You are so stubborn and you didn't get that from me." He chuckled trying to keep from crying.

"I know, I know. I'm not a badass, and I take after my mother. What are you gonna do with me?" I tried to laugh which caused more pain and made me cry. Seeing me cry Logan sat on the bed and put his arm around me. I smiled through my tears thinking that even with a possible broken nose, I had never been this happy in my entire life. I looked up at Logan, kissed his cheek, and whispered, "Thank you!"

"Thank you for what? I'm the one who took you to the bar. This is kind of my fault." He couldn't help but blame himself.

"You didn't make those assholes get drunk and fight. Nor did you make that bastard miss his target and punch me. Except for the whole being in pain and in the emergency room, this has been the perfect night. I say next time we just have a picnic or something. Is that okay with you?" I suggested with a half smile.

"That sounds like a brilliant plan. I promise no emergency room visits next time. That is if you still want to see me again after this."

"I'm not letting a little punch in the face by a stranger

ruin my night." I giggled and winced from the pain.

The doctor interrupted us. "That was more than just a little punch. I'm sorry to tell you that your nose is broken. The nurse will be in soon to give you some meds before I cause more pain fixing it."

"Just what I needed. A broken nose. Guess you get to drive me to Kansas City Dad." I tried to laugh it off.

"Don't worry about it Hon. I'll get you there, help you pack, and get you back here. I know I'm old, but I can still drive you know," he joked.

I fought through the pain as we all laughed. A few minutes later the nurse came in with a shot for the pain and I cringed when I saw the needle. Logan noticed and held my hand while I unhappily endured the "small" pinch and horrible burning sensation. About ten minutes later the doctor walked in and started to fix my nose. All I could remember the next morning was extreme pain, passing out a few times, and parts of the ride home. When I looked into the mirror I had to fight the tears, because I looked so bad. I was positive Logan was never going to want to see me again. When I walked out of my room to get some breakfast, I noticed Logan asleep on the couch and my dad in his recliner. The television was still on and it looked like they fell asleep talking. I barely made it into the kitchen when I felt arms around my waist. I turned to see Logan standing there.

"How are you feeling this morning?" he kissed my forehead.

"Like I was punched in the face." We both laughed.

As he started to reply, the home phone rang making both of us jump and I hit my nose on his arm.

"Hello?" I said trying not to cry.

"Hello Brooke. It's Chief Parks. I was calling to see if you knew where Logan was. He didn't show up for work and isn't answering his phone."

I looked up at Logan and smiled. "Yes Chief I do happen to know where your missing officer is. In fact he happens to be standing in front of me right now." A look of fear crossed Logan's face. He kissed my forehead, grabbed his keys, and ran out of the house.

"Why is he at your house and not at work?" he said angrily.

"Well, things turned bad last night. After dinner we went to a bar. Two men started fighting. Long story short we spent most of the night in the emergency room and my nose is broken. I assure you he is on his way home to change and get to work. He was so worried and tired he fell asleep on the couch. It's my fault so please go easy on him," I begged.

"I'll let it slide this time since you were hurt last night. Next time I'll have to write him up. Take care of yourself and try to have a great day." He hung up before I could say anything else.

I gathered everything needed to make breakfast and started cooking. Just before I finished cooking, Dad woke up and there was a knock on the door. I asked Dad to get it so the food wouldn't burn. I got breakfast finished and plated, but before I could take them to the table, I saw two familiar hands reach around me to grab the plates. I turned and smiled seeing Logan's face. It was a nice surprise.

"Why aren't you at work? You're going to get in trouble," I scolded him.

"The Chief said he couldn't have a half asleep officer out patrolling and told me to go home and get some sleep. I didn't want to go home so I came back here. Is that okay?"

"That's fine with me. I only made enough food for two though. I guess you'll have to share with my dad," I giggled.

"He is not sharing with me. I just made a call and I'm going to meet Ethan and Frank for breakfast. The two of you can have breakfast, then both of you need some sleep. I'll pick up your meds on my way home. They sent a pill home with you last night. Take it after you eat. Logan," he said in his stern fatherly voice, "no funny business with my daughter in my house. You got it?"

"I promise. Nothing above a 'G' rating in this house." He nodded his head.

"Go eat Dad!" I shouted in embarrassment. "I want to eat while my food is still warm."

We sat at the table but I found it hard to eat. I watched Logan shovel the food into his mouth as I pushed my food around on the plate. After he finished his bacon and eggs, I took the plates to the sink to wash them. He stood next to me holding a glass of orange juice and a pain pill while impatiently tapping his foot.

"Relax, I'll take it in a few minutes. I need to wash these plates. Do you know how hard it is to get dried egg yolk off of dishes?" I whined.

"Take your pill and go lay down. I can wash the plates for you. You need as much rest as possible. I'll come in and check on you when I'm done," he insisted.

"Fine, but those plates better be spotless or your nose will be just as broken." I took the pill and stormed off to my room like an angry two year old. I threw myself on the bed, covered up, and stared off into space. After a few minutes I stared at my alarm clock, full of boredom. It took Logan 20 minutes to finish the dishes and come check on me. I looked at him with my sad puppy dog eyes and said,

"My nose hurts and I can't sleep. Will you tell me a story?" I tried so hard to keep a straight face.

Logan laughed so hard he had tears streaming down his face. "Poor baby, what story would you like to hear?"

I stuck out my bottom lip and pouted trying to act as sad as possible. "Tell me the story about the moron who was too stupid to move away from the grown ass drunken men that were fighting, and got herself knocked out. Tell me how she ruined her first date with an amazing man."

He went from laughing to having the sweetest smile on his face. He crawled in bed next me, pulled me close, and snuggled up. "Okay, but I don't think that's how it ended. Once upon a time, or yesterday, I can't remember all of the details, a beautiful woman took charge and asked the man she was interested in out. He picked her up later that night and took her out to dinner. What he didn't tell her was that he was a ball of nerves the entire time. After dinner he took his sexy date to a bar for a night of drinks and dancing. They were both laughing and having a wonderful night, when two men started to fight next to them. The man was too slow and failed to protect his date and she got severely injured. This crushed the man's heart. He rushed his princess to the nearest emergency room hoping to make up for his failure. After he got her fixed up and home, he sat on the couch all night talking to her father about how sorry he was for failing and how he would never forgive himself. The father explained that it wasn't his fault and that he shouldn't be so hard on himself. After a couple of hours of talking, both men fell asleep until the princess, in all her pain, got up to fix a wonderful breakfast. It was then that the man knew he would forever love and protect the princess. The End!"

I couldn't even speak. All I could do is look up at him, cry, kiss his soft lips, and snuggle closer. I fell asleep in his arms and several hours later I woke up in them. I wanted to stay like that forever and never leave his arms. I felt safe, loved, and protected. When I looked up he was staring at me and smiling.

"Did you watch me the whole time I slept? That's kind of creepy. This princess is not into stalkers." I laughed as my dad walked into the room to make sure we were following his rules. "Chill Dad, no funny business here. Well, except I think Logan might be a creepy stalker. He watched me sleep all day."

My dad found this extremely funny. "No dear he didn't. When I got home 20 minutes ago he was asleep. He's not a stalker. Now get up and come have some lunch. I got your favorite from the diner. Come on lazy bones you need to eat."

I grumbled and muttered under my breath before getting out of bed. "Why can't I have lunch in my nice comfy bed? Am I not in enough pain and discomfort for you?" I stuck out my tongue.

When I got to the table, Uncle David and Chief Parks were sitting there. I sighed and sat down reluctantly. They stared at me in shock before turning to Logan with questions in their eyes. I know they blamed him for how horrible I looked, but I could only blame myself. I was proud of how he reacted. He could have left me on the floor and gone after the two men, but instead was quickly by my side. He got me the help I needed and stayed close to me all night.

"Don't you dare look at Logan like that," I snapped. "He did what he could and got me to the emergency room. He kept his cool and didn't kill the guys. Besides it was my fault for not moving further away from them. I knew better."

"Why didn't you stop the fight before it got out of hand?" the Chief asked Logan a little too harshly.

"It all happened so fast. The two men started fighting. I tried to go over and stop them and Brooke was punched. I had to help her before I did anything else. I already feel guilty. Please don't point out how much I failed." Logan cried and placed his head in his hands.

I stood up full of rage, placed my hands on my hips, and started going off. "You have no right to come in here and blame him for anything. If you can't be nice and respectful, I suggest you both get the fuck out of here." I sat back down feeling dizzy and proud of myself.

"Where did that come from?" my dad asked full of shock.

"I'm sorry. I just can't accept you putting the blame on Logan. It's not his fault." My eyes started to fill with tears and my whole face started throbbing.

Chief Parks looked at us with guilt written all over his face. "I shouldn't have been so harsh. I apologize. This is not why we came here. We have to tell you about a threat on your life."

"My life was threatened? I don't understand why. What did I do wrong? Who threatened me?"

"We got an anonymous letter in the mail today. The letter said that if you continue to interview Clara and try to find out the truth about your mother, that the person will kill you and your father. Until further notice there will be an officer placed outside of the house and each one of you will have a temporary bodyguard," Uncle David tried to comfort me.

"What about my trip to Kansas City? I need to get my stuff moved back here," I pleaded.

"You can still go. You just need to take someone with who can keep you safe," Chief Parks said. "Logan you will accompany Ms. Stevens to Kansas City? We want you to report to us and the local police department if you see anyone or anything suspicious. We already called and made arrangements for you to do whatever is needed to protect her. Under the circumstances the sooner you leave town, the better. You're father will remain here under our protection and we will call with updates so you don't worry as much. Logan please go home and pack. We will watch Brooke until you return."

I gave Logan another kiss and he rushed out to get his stuff needed for the trip. While he was gone I headed to my room to start packing. It took longer than I thought it would and I was overcome with tears. Why would anyone want me dead? It just proved my theory about Clara knowing the truth about my mom's murder. I finished packing, set my bags next to the door, and waited silently for Logan to return.

Chapter Eight

On the drive to Kansas City neither Logan nor I talked much. I plugged in my MP3 player and we quietly listened to music. We were both in so much shock we didn't know what to say. We both blamed ourselves for the incident and now my life was in danger. All I wanted to do was help the police and finally know what happened to my mother. I sat staring out my window watching the trees and houses race by. I tried my hardest to keep my emotions in check, but as the song Wanted by Hunter Hayes came on and Logan started singing to me, I gave in and let the tears flow. I knew deep down that there was a chance Logan would have to live without me. There was also a chance he could get hurt or die. I never knew I could love someone so much so quickly. I couldn't imagine my life without him and wondered how I made it this far not knowing him.

"I love you Logan Galloway!" I sobbed.

"I love you too Brooke Stevens! Nothing in this world will ever change that and I promise to do everything in my power to keep you safe until the world ends." He reached over and squeezed my hand.

Hearing his words somehow made me relax a bit. For the last hour we sang along to the music and danced in our seats. We laughed and made fun of each other's dancing. Once we made it to the city I directed him on how to get to my parking garage. I stopped by the manager's office to get any overflow mail and talk to him about my moving. He said he was sad to see his best tenant leave, but wished me well. I told him I knew it would be after the first of the month when I would be leaving so I would make sure to get the rent check to him in the morning. The manager smiled and I led Logan up to my apartment.

"Well, here it is. My tiny little apartment. Would you like a tour?" I snickered.

"Wow! You live here, in this tiny little apartment? Is there even a bathroom or closets, or are they communal?" he made fun of my cute little apartment.

"Oh hush," I playfully snapped back at him. "It was the perfect place for just me. Besides I was rarely even home. All I did was work, so what did I need a big expensive apartment for? Now set the bags down and follow me." I grabbed his hand and walked him around the apartment. "This is the kitchen where I make the best food in the world. Over here is my tiny table for two. Through that door is the bathroom and the closet. This is my desk, where all the wonderful words are written. Finally, this is my bed which is way too big for this little apartment." I pushed him onto the bed and walked away. "Isn't it comfy? I'm gonna get a glass of water would you like some?"

"First of all, yes the bed is comfy. Second of all, it would be even better with you in it." He winked and patted the bed next to him trying to get me to join him.

"You're too funny. I can't 'sleep' until I take my meds. I can't take my meds until I eat. I already sent a mass text to all my friends. We will meet them in about 30 minutes at Nara NeoJapanese. They have the best sushi in town. Now take your bag and go change. I want you to meet all of my wonderful friends."

I quickly changed my shirt, when I noticed the bathroom

door cracked open. I forgot to tell him he had to pull it closed pretty hard. I couldn't help but stare at his shirtless, perfectly chiseled chest while he shaved. A wave of excitement hit me when I realized he saw me staring. Blushing, I quickly turned away and went into the kitchen for another glass of ice cold water.

He sauntered shirtless out of the bathroom. "Who's the creepy stalker now? Do you like what you see?" he walked over and pulled me into the deepest, most passionate kiss I ever had in my life. It caused my heart to skip a beat and I melted in his arms.

"Stop that. You're distracting me and I don't like that." I started walking away but found myself not wanting to. I turned back around and kissed him again. Unfortunately the kiss didn't last long. I pulled back gasping for air. "Maybe we should wait until my nose works again. I can't breathe when my nose is plugged up, and your wonderfully, delicious lips are pressed up against mine. Let's finish getting ready so we aren't too late."

"I guess I see your point," he sulked. "It just won't be any fun if you pass out on me. I'll grab my shirt and gun, and then we can go. Don't worry. I'll leave it in the car if it makes you feel better."

"It won't bother me, but there is a no gun policy where we are going."

I watched him put a shirt on and felt saddened that I could no longer see his sexy abs. I grabbed my keys and we headed out for the night. This time he let me drive since I actually knew where I was going. We arrived at the restaurant and all my friends were waiting. The women all stared at Logan with looks of jealousyand the men looked at him in anger after noticing my nose.

"What the hell happened to your nose?" Josh half yelled.

"Who's the hottie beside you?" Victoria exclaimed.

"Relax; we have all night to talk about my horrible looking deformity. We also have plenty of time to talk about my nose," I joked looking at Logan. The table burst into laughter as Logan and I took our seats. "Everyone this is my boyfriend/bodyguard, Officer Logan Galloway. Before you ask, no, he did not break my nose. We were at a bar last night when two men started fighting. The man who was supposed to get the fist to the face moved and I was standing a little too close. I'm fine, and my hero over here got me right to the hospital."

Everyone said their hellos and introduced themselves before Mandy asked, "You said he was also your bodyguard. Why do you need a bodyguard?"

"Well as my emails said I am interviewing the serial killer in Brines. I thought she had information about my mother's murder. Earlier today the police station got an anonymous letter threatening to kill me and my father if I didn't stop looking into my mother's death. So we headed here and Logan was assigned as my bodyguard. They knew I would have refused anyone else. So here we are."

We ate dinner, talked, and caught up on everything I missed since I had left. To my surprise Logan jumped right in on the conversation. It was as if he had always known everyone. It made me love him even more. We stayed until the restaurant closed at midnight, said goodbye, and headed back to the apartment. I immediately took my meds, changed into my comfies, and got all snuggled up in bed and ready to sleep.

"We need to go get boxes tomorrow and then I need to start packing. I love seeing my friends, but I'm too worried about dad to stay here a week."

"I understand, but you know he's safe. They won't let

him out of their sight. I promise. Try and relax while I go change." He went to the bathroom to change. "If you really want to speed pack I'll help. We can pack tomorrow and I'll take you back home the next day. It is a lot safer for you here, but we can head home soon." He laid down next to me, pulled me in close, and we drifted off to sleep.

In the morning we woke up to knocking on the door. Logan jumped up and grabbed his gun before making his way to the door. He motioned for me to come over and whispered, "Calmly ask who it is."

"Who is it?" I yawned.

"It's Josh and the gang. We came to help you get all packed."

Logan lowered his gun, and gave me the okay to open the door. I was so glad it was them and not some psychopath trying to kill me.

"We come bearing boxes and lots of donuts. You get to supply the coffee, the items to pack, and one sexy chiseled man to stare at - a man that's holding a gun. Should we be worried?" Angela asked confused.

"We were sleeping when you came banging on the door. With everything going on, we didn't know if it was someone coming to kill me or what." I turned to Logan and frowned, "Put that thing away before you give us all heart attacks."

Logan looked at the gun he was still holding. "I'm so sorry. I guess none of you want to kill Brooke. I'll put it away and make everyone some coffee. Then we can all start packing."

It was a tight fit at first, while we all stood around eating and joking. For a moment in time I actually forgot that my life was in danger. It only took a few hours to get everything packed so we decided to go to lunch and show Logan our favorite places in town. We opted out of driving and chose to walk around for a few hours. I called and reserved a U-Haul for the next morning while we ate. For me the day went by so fast I couldn't even remember what we did by the time we returned to the apartment. I wrote out a check for rent and handed it to the landlord before heading up the stairs. I took my meds and went to sleep without dinner.

I was up early in the morning to finish packing any last minute items, and go pick up the U-haul. I left without waking Logan, but I left him a note telling him where I went in case he woke up. By the time I returned, Logan was awake and my friends were there to help load everything in. I gave Logan a "don't start with me" look, and he seemed to get it. We loaded up, said goodbye to my friends, and hit the road for home.

Chapter Nine

For the first hour, all we did was argue. He was mad that I left the apartment without him and I was mad that he was treating me like a fragile child.

"I can't believe you did that. Have you lost your mind?" he yelled.

"I'm not a fucking child. I can handle picking up a U-haul without someone holding my damn hand. Besides, if you haven't noticed the police have been following me everywhere. I know the police here from my job at the paper. They wouldn't let me get hurt," I spat.

"I don't know them, nor do I trust them. We don't know who threatened you, or who they might know. You have to be more careful. I just found you and I don't want to lose you. Do you understand?"

"I get where you're coming from. I don't want to lose you either, but I can't put my life on hold. The note was probably from one of the stupid churches that think I'm trying to glorify what Clara did."

"Why would you think that?"

"Because, four days ago I got an email from a member of one of the churches telling me just that."

"Why didn't you tell Chief Parks about the email?"

"I didn't think about it until this morning. I'm sorry, but

I'm not going to let them stop me. If there is even the smallest hope of finding clues about my mother, I have to try. Do you get what I'm saying?"

"I do understand. Please let me help keep you safe though. I'm not saying you can't handle yourself. I know you can. All I'm saying is that it's my job to help keep you safe."

"It's your job? Why, because you're the big strong man, and I'm the weak helpless woman?" I retorted.

"Jesus Christ Brooke!" He shouted. "It has nothing to do with being a man or a woman. It's because I'm a police officer. I literally get paid to protect people."

We both started laughing knowing both of us had great points to make, and both of us were wrong.

"Do you realize we just had our first fight?" I giggled, glad that it was over.

"Well that was an easy fight. Glad we got that out of the way. I say we make up as soon as we get you moved into your own house." He grinned and winked at me.

I grabbed his hand and sweetly replied, "I vote we make up at your place tonight."

"I concur." He flashed his pearly whites at me. "Look at that, we agreed on something today."

"Don't get used to it mister. I may have to disagree more often if we end fights like that," I admitted to him.

"Let's promise to fight and make up every day. Do we have a deal?"

"I can agree with that. Now hurry up and drive faster. I'd like to see for myself that my dad is safe."

About half way home we stopped to get some food. I wanted to just go through a drive-thru, but he wanted to eat somewhere that's not moving. We settled on an I-HOP.

After eating we got back on the road and listened to music the rest of the way. This time we listened to his music, which was not easy. Some of the songs weren't in English and the rest was classical. I was pretty sure he was trying to get me to sleep the rest of the trip. We pulled up in front of Dad's house and I ran in to see him. As per usual he was napping on the couch.

"Wake up daddy. I'm home, I'm home!" I shouted like a little kid.

He jumped up scared not realizing at first who I was. When he noticed it was me he wrapped his arms around me.

"It's so good to see you, but why are you home so soon?"

"I was worried about you and didn't want you to be gone for a week or two. You know how I am."

"Where's Logan? Did the two of you have a fight? Did you leave him somewhere on the side of the road?" he laughed knowing how stubborn I am.

"We did have a fight, but that's over. Also, yes, I did leave him somewhere. I left him outside with your bodyguards. Is that okay with you?"

"I guess, but what did you fight about?"

"Nothing important, let's not dwell on it. What did you do while I was gone? Did you fall in love and get married?" I teased.

"You won't ever give up on that will you?"

"Nope, sorry, I need my dad to be happy."

"I spent my time being lazy for once. What did you do? Are you married yet, or are you working on becoming an old maid?"

"We totally got married. He thought we should wait so you could be there. I said the hell with that, I don't want to wait. Let's just do it now and get this shit over with." We burst into laughter as Logan entered the room.

"Did I miss something?" he asked.

"Not much honey. I just told Dad about us getting married in Kansas City, that's all."

"Um….. Okay!" he said confused. "Did I sleep through my own wedding? Man you drugged me didn't you?" he tried to play along.

"Well you weren't going to ask, so I slipped you a mickey. Don't be such a girl about it," I joked as Chief Parks walked in looking slightly amused and confused.

"You better not have gotten married. You can't do that without a bachelor party first. You know with strippers and lots of drinking."

"No on the strippers Chief Parks. Don't make me hurt you. I'm a badass remember?" I tried to keep a straight face but failed miserably.

"We aren't married at this time I promise. If I propose I promise we will tell everyone," I explained to the chief.

"Wait!" Logan held up his hand. "If you propose? I thought that was my job?"

"Why are we even discussing marriage?" I tried to change the conversation. "Any information on who sent the letter yet? I'd like to move into my new house and get back to work"

"The lab ran every test possible and we can't find anything. No prints, no DNA, no nothing," Jackson said looking disappointed.

"Maybe Clara will know who sent it. I'll ask her tomorrow. For now, let's all go out and get some food. Logan, can you ask Dad's guards what they want us to bring back for them?"

"I'm on it boss," he yelled as he headed out the front door.

With a list of food in hand we headed to our cars, when a loud bang had us all throwing ourselves to the ground. The officer that had been standing by the front door raised his gun and shot across the street towards the neighbor's house. We looked over in time to see a figure drop to the ground. The other officer ran across the street to see if the man was still alive while we all got up and checked each other for bullet wounds. I hit my nose when I dropped to the ground causing it to bleed. Logan noticed but as he started to get up, he was stopped by a sharp pain in his abdomen. I noticed him cringe and ran over to help.

"Chief Parks, Logan was hit! We need to get him to the hospital!" I lost control and panic set in.

We rushed around to get Logan safely in a car and got him to the hospital as the other officer's started blocking off the crime scene and shutting down access to the road. At the hospital Logan was taken back to see a doctor and I paced the waiting room, filled with tears and worry. They wouldn't allow anyone to go back with him. After an hour a nurse came out and told me that before Logan was taken to surgery he insisted that someone look at my still bleeding nose. He had just been shot and was still more worried about my well being than his own.

"I'm fine!" I insisted. The nurse however disagreed and took me back to see a doctor. I was forced to go through more x-rays to determine what I already knew. They never listen to the patient these days. They put new bandages on my nose and I was sent back to the waiting room. I continued to pace for a couple more hours before the surgeon finally came out to speak with us.

"Officer Galloway is doing fine. The bullet missed all of his vital organs. It nicked a major artery, but I was able to repair it and stop the bleeding." The doctor had a look of relief on his face.

"When can I see him?" I asked impatiently.

"While he's in the ICU only family can see him. I'm sorry, but you'll have to wait," he admitted.

"He doesn't have any family here andis parents live 10 hours away," the chief explained.

"Please let me see him," I pleaded. "I don't want him to be alone when he wakes up. I'm his girlfriend, doesn't that matter?"

"It's hospital pol…." he tried to tell us but was interrupted.

"Fuck your policies!" my dad yelled. "Just let my daughter go back and be with him or you'll have to answer to me."

We all turned to look at my dad when the doctor finally agreed to let me see Logan. I had never been more proud of my father than at that moment. A few minutes of walking felt like an eternity to me as I was led back to the ICU. I sat next to Logan's bed, kissed his hand, and waited quietly with my head lying next to him on the bed. I couldn't help but think that this was my fault. Maybe I should have given up on the interviews and the truth about my mother. Was it really worth losing the people I love? Logan survived this time, but what's to say he would make it next time. What about my dad? I couldn't let anyone else get hurt because of my stubbornness. I had almost cried myself to sleep when I felt a hand brush the top of my head. I looked up to see Logan smiling down at me.

"You didn't think a little bullet could keep us apart did you?" He tried to laugh but it caused more pain.

"I was so worried about you. I just found you and I'm not letting go so easily. Besides being shot, how are you feeling? Do you need anything? I'll go get the nurse at the desk. She wanted to know when you woke up if she wasn't already in here."

"Slow down Brooke. I'm in pain, but I can handle it. I just want to have a few minutes alone with you before they kick you out and cause more pain. Just sit here with me and hold my hand. Please."

I did as he asked. Before I had a chance to do much of anything the nurse came in to see how he was doing. When she noticed he was awake she left the room to call the doctor. At least we got a few more minutes alone before everyone started rushing in to make sure there were no complications. I was once again ushered out of the room and into the waiting area where half of the Brines Police Department was gathered around talking. When they saw me enter with tears in my eyes, they all started to think the worst. I was quickly surrounded with questions being thrown at me left and right.

"What's wrong?" my dad asked.

"Nothing, I'm just a big ole cry baby tonight. He's awake and they are checking him out."

"So those are happy tears?" one of the officers asked.

"Yes and no. I'm happy he's awake, but I'm pissed off that they kicked me out of the room. I know they need to make sure he's okay, but I still don't have to be happy about it."

Everyone started laughing which only fueled my rage. I

hated being laughed at, and I hated showing my weakness even more. I walked away from the group and headed for the vending machine. I decided I might as well eat something while I waited. Plus it was nice to get away from the group. I slipped into a different waiting area, determined to avoid all people until I could go back to Logan's side. I sat on the floor in the corner of the dark room, and it was peaceful. After a few minutes I heard their voices calling out my name. I heard the rush of feet and the fear in their voices. I laughed knowing it was their turn to be full of panic and fear. I won this battle. Uncle David found me after about an hour of searching. He was furious with me for not coming out when I heard my name being called.

"Have you lost your damn mind? You know you can't run off like that. We have been looking everywhere for you and you almost gave your father a heart attack."

"I'm sorry, but I needed to be alone. I can't handle being followed everywhere all the time. I'm sure that if you were in my place, you would do the same thing."

"I understand, but that doesn't give you the right to walk away from us. The shooter was not after you and only hit one of his targets. He had nothing to do with the letter we got. He was an angry 16 year old boy looking to get revenge for the arrest of his parents. The person targeting you and your father is still out there and we have no idea who it is. Next time, tell us you want to be alone and although we will still guard you, we will give you more space." His voice was full of anger and concern.

"Alright, I promise I won't wander off into anymore empty rooms without telling you first. Can I go back and see Logan yet?"

"The doctor is waiting to talk to you. I'm sure he will let you go back afterwards. Let's go let your father know you're safe, and then find that doctor," David suggested.

I followed him to where my father sat crying and my heart sank. "I'm okay dad. I am so sorry that I scared you. I just needed to get away from everyone. Please don't be mad at me. Next time I promise to let you know where I am going."

"You scared me half to death. I thought someone kidnapped you, and I'd never see you again. If you ever do that to me again, I will find you and kick your ass myself." He hugged me so tight and I could tell he was afraid to let go.

"I need to find the doctor and get back to Logan. He needs someone there until his parents arrive. I'll keep an officer with me at all times. I promise."

He finally let go of me and I asked a nurse to get the doctor for me. When he arrived he told me that Logan seemed to be holding up just fine and took me to his new room to see him. I carefully crawled into bed and snuggled up with Logan. We both drifted off into a much needed and very peaceful sleep. Neither of us woke when the nurse came in to check his vitals or do his blood work. We slept until the next morning when his parents came rushing into the room. I crawled out of bed and moved aside to give his parents space to see him. As I made my way to the door so they could have some privacy his mother grabbed my arm and stopped me.

"Are you Brooke?" she asked.

"I am. I'll give you both some time alone with your son." I smiled. "He's a wonderful man, and you should be proud of him."

"We are always proud of him. Thank you for making sure he wasn't alone. That means so much to us."

"I will never let him be alone. He's my everything." With that that I left the room.

I was met in the waiting room by David and he walked with me to the cafeteria. We sat for a few hours eating and talking. We discussed the young man who shot Logan, and my wanting to give up on the interviews.

"I have never known you to give up on anything. When backed into a corner, you always fight back."

"That's true except this time not backing down could kill the people I love the most. I can't let that happen. Even if it means showing how weak I truly am. I couldn't live with myself if anyone was hurt or killed because I was too stubborn. You won't make me change my mind. Not now, not ever," I said stubbornly.

"You are your mother's daughter. She was just as stubborn as you if not more so. I won't fight you on this. I only hope you come to your senses."

"I've made my decision. If you'll excuse me, I am going back to Logan's room now. Come find me if you get any more information."

I made it halfway back to the room when Chief Parks and several officers ran up and surrounded me. They quickly walked me back to Logan's room, pushed me inside, and closed the door. I looked at Logan and his parents filled with sheer terror. I knew something was wrong, but no one was saying a word. I sat next to Logan shaking in fear and lost all control. A moment later Chief Parks barged into the room and headed straight for me.

"Until further notice you are not to leave this room. I went to check on your father this morning and found the front door guard lying dead in a pool of blood. I rushed in to find your father face down on the table. This is not how I wanted to tell you. Your father is dead. I am so sorry we couldn't protect him. We are doing everything possible to find the person responsible," he tried to assure me.

I dropped to my knees and erupted into a fit of tears. The last of my family was dead, and it was all my fault. If I had of listened to my dad to begin with he'd still be alive. Chief Parks tried to comfort me, but I pushed him away. There was nothing he or anyone else could say or do to make the pain in my heart go away. I could not be convinced that this wasn't my fault. I did this. I was the cause of my father's murder. I would stop at nothing to find the person responsible, and bring them to justice. It was my new mission in life. Chief Parks left the room, while Logan's parents came over to comfort me. They didn't talk, or try to get me to move from my spot on the floor. Without a word his mother and father just held me. They knew it was all I needed at the time. I was there for their son when he needed me most and now they would do the same for me.

After an hour of crying I fell asleep. Logan's dad picked me up and placed me next to Logan so I'd be more comfortable, and Logan could take over being there for me. He was still holding on to me when I woke up screaming from a nightmare. Hearing my scream an officer rushed into the room. Logan waved for him to leave knowing that the officer's presence might upset me more. Forgetting about Logan's injury, I rolled over and held him tighter. I began to cry again and he quietly stroked my hair. He didn't know what to say so he didn't say anything at all. It broke his heart to see me so hurt and upset. All he wanted to do was take away all of my pain and bring back my smile.

The four of us spent an entire week in Logan's hospital room. It depressed me that I couldn't even make arrangements for my father's funeral. Uncle David handled everything for me. I decided to have him cremated and to arrange a memorial service for him after it was once again safe. Our only visitors were a couple of nurses, the doctor, and a few random officers bringing us food and games to play. When I wasn't eating or sleeping I was sitting on the floor staring into space. I remembered how close my dad and I got after my mother's death, and how hard it was to go off to college and get my first real job. I remembered how he questioned my first date before letting me leave and how over protective he had been my whole life. I hated it back then and I'd give anything to have that feeling again. To have any feeling at all would have been a miracle. I was so numb to my emotions. I knew I loved Logan, but I refused to let myself feel it. I pushed away from him in hopes of making it easier in the event I lost him too.

When the doctor finally said Logan could go home, his apartment was searched and he was quickly taken with his parents to their new temporary prison. I refused to go with them and stayed in a hotel alone instead. In my mind I was convinced that he was safer without me. Uncle David tried to get me to stay with them, but I refused. I was never going to put anyone else in harm's way.

"Staying with you would just put your lives in danger. I can't have anyone else die because of me. I just need some clothes and my computer. I need to start making funeral arrangements. Just bring my stuff here, and leave me alone."

"I can't just leave you alone. You're my family, and I can't walk away. No matter how angry it makes you, or how much you fight me on this. We will bring you your stuff and some food. Try to get some rest. I'll be back in an hour or so."

I turned on the television to get my mind on something else. There was a knock on the door and I realized I had been flipping through the channels for over an hour. Feeling nervous I asked who it was. I was beyond relieved to hear Uncle David's voice on the other side. I unlocked the door and let him in. As we sat and ate dinner, I almost felt normal. That is until we were interrupted with a Breaking News report on TV. We stopped and stared as they announced that another dead body was found. The reporter explained that the body of a homeless man was found tortured and dumped on the side of the road. It was the same type of torture as the bodies found on the night of August 29th. We sat shocked, realizing that Clara must have had an accomplice or we had a copycat on our hands. I turned off the TV and David got up to leave. He gave me a hug and promised to do whatever was needed to keep me safe. At that moment I knew I had to talk to Clara again. I had to make her admit that she didn't do it alone. She had help and I knew it.

I turned on my computer and franticly looked over my files. I had to see if she gave any clues about anyone who may have helped her. I spent the entire night listening to the interviews and reading over my files. To my disappointment I found no proof. That meant I had to go see her again. No matter what the cost, I had to get the answers. I couldn't let this go any longer. I showered, dressed, and called the chief to let him know I was on my way. Despite his arguments about me leaving the hotel, I ignored him and told one of the officers to give me a ride to the station.

Chapter Ten

Knowing full well I was on my way to the station the chief had Clara brought up to one of the interview rooms. Her lawyer was called and gave his permission for me to do the interview without him in the room. I was silent the entire ride. All I could do was think of what questions I had for her, while trying to calm myself enough that I wouldn't strangle her right there in the room. I was greeted by the officers with looks of sadness and sympathy. I ignored them and walked straight into the room. I was a woman on a mission and no one was going to get in my way.

I tried to get set up as calmly as possible, but Clara could see the fire brewing in my eyes.

"I don't have time for games. I am here for answers and I want them now. So help me God, if you try to play any of your games not one officer in this room will be able to save your life."

"What happened to you? You've changed and I don't like this side of you."

"Not long ago a letter was sent to the police chief. The letter warned that if I didn't stop interviewing you and give up on finding the truth about my mother, that my father and I would be killed. So far Logan was shot and they are trying to convince me it was unrelated. A week ago the two officers guarding my dad were shot, and my father was found murdered at his dining room table. I want to know who sent that letter and why they killed my father when I hadn't even talked to you in over a week. Start talking now," I demanded with enough anger in my voice that even Clara looked petrified.

"I don't know who sent the letter. They already questioned me about it. The only person I can think of is my father. I was going to wait until after I told you about all of my victims before telling you what I know about your mother's death. I want a promise that even after I tell you what I know, you will still come back and hear my story."

She shrank in her seat a bit as she tried to get me to agree to her terms. I could tell she was scared and even a little nervous.

"Fine, I promise after you tell me the truth and we find the person responsible, I will continue with the interviews. Now start talking. I want the truth."

She looked at the floor and trembled as she spoke. "About ten years ago my mother was forced into rehab. I didn't want to be in the system, so I lied and said my dad received treatment for his anger and they let me stay with him. Things were really bad, but I knew it was only going to last a few months. By then I would be 18 and could live wherever I wanted. Aside from the daily beatings, I had to watch many different women come and go from my dad's house. Occasionally I was forced to watch him beat the women and have sex with them. None of the women ever spoke a word about it, because my father would threaten to kill their loved ones. I was too afraid to speak up."

"What does any of this have to do with my mother? You're wearing thin on my patience. Get to the point!" I screamed inches from her face.

"I promise it has a lot to do with your mother. Three

weeks before my birthday I witnessed a young woman about my age running from the house. I didn't know who she was or what he did to her, but I knew she was terrified. My father ran out of his room bleeding and yelled for me to get her and bring her back. I couldn't bring myself to do it. I froze in place even though I knew I would pay for it, but it was better me than her, right?" she asked saddened by the thought.

"Get on with it already. You're not getting any pity from me."

"A couple of days later the police arrived to question my father and try to get me to talk. He had me chained up and locked in the basement. When they got no answers from him, they asked to speak to me. I heard my father tell them that I had run away from home and he didn't know where I was. They were stupid enough to believe him and left the house. I was labeled a runaway and the young girl a liar. I finally managed to convince him that I would keep my mouth shut and that I would tell the police anything he wanted. I don't know why, but he agreed."

"Why didn't you tell the police when you spoke to them? They would have protected you."

"I was a broken young woman by then. The police had failed to protect me so far. I was convinced they would keep failing me and I would end up dead. I went to the station to give my statement. I explained the cuts and bruising by saying I had been jumped by a group of boys at a park, and didn't remember who they were. I also told them I was with my dad the entire night in question and never saw anybody else at the house. I must have been convincing enough since they let me leave and go back to my dad's. As I was leaving, I bumped into your mother, who was bringing lunch to the officers. She asked me about my bruises. I said I didn't want to talk about it and ran back home. I hoped she would leave it alone, but I was wrong. I was so wrong."

"So my mother was a concerned woman. We all know how she was. She'd protect anyone from anything. What did she do that was bad enough to get her killed?"

"She showed up with the Department of Family Services the next day. They did a walkthrough of the entire house except for the basement. My dad said my mom had locked it several years earlier and he never found the key. As usual they bought every word he said. They asked about my many cuts and bruises and I told them basically the same story I told the police. They left after determining there was no abuse and that my dad was a changed man. Your mother however, didn't buy it. She came back an hour later and asked to come in and spend some time with me. I couldn't convince her to leave. She spent all afternoon with me and left knowing she couldn't prove anything, but that something wasn't right. Later that night a loud thud from downstairs woke me up."

"Was it my mother?" I asked.

"It was. My dad had her gagged and was dragging her to the basement by her hair. He threw her down the stairs, grabbed my arm, and forced me into the basement with them. He chained me to a pole, and tied your mother to his work table. I screamed for him to let her go, but instead he hit me with so much force that I was knocked unconscious." She couldn't hold it in anymore and started to cry.

I felt bad for her, but something didn't seem right. It was almost as if the tears were faked. Like she was trying force a reaction out of me. I didn't know what to think.

"Now I know where the monster inside you comes from. You are just as evil as he is." It took everything I had inside of me to keep from beating her.

"I am so sorry. I tried to get your mother to drop it. I tried so hard to convince her I was alright. I failed her and I failed myself. Should I continue?"

"Yes, I have to know how she died."

"When I came to, she was badly beaten and my father was raping her. I couldn't get to him to stop the horrible act and my mouth was glued shut. All I could do was close my eyes and cry. This went on for almost two days before she died. He started by making small cuts all over her body, but when it came time for the kill he grabbed a gun, unchained me, placed a knife in my hand, and told me to end her suffering or he would end it himself along with my life and your mother's. I didn't want to kill her, but I didn't want to die either. After staring into your mothers eyes and seeing her beg me to do it, I did. I stabbed the knife into her heart and watched the life drain from her eyes."

Hearing that Clara had killed my mother made my blood begin to boil. Before I knew what I was doing, I had jumped up, leaped over the table, and started to strangle her. I managed to not be phased by the officers' taser in my side, knocked him to the ground, and continued to beat on her until two more officers came in and subdued me. They cuffed me to a chair in the chief's office while they escorted Clara back to her cell. After about thirty minutes of cursing and yelling to let me go, Logan came into the room. He grabbed my face and forced me to look at him.

"You have to calm down. Tell me what happened in there."

"She killed my mother. That worthless bitch and her father killed my mother. If she had told the police the truth 10 years ago, my mother would still be alive. I want that bitch dead for what she did!" I screamed while shaking uncontrollably.

"How did she kill your mother? What did she lie to the police about? I need to know or I can't help you."

"She lied to the police, my mother, and the Department of Family Services. My mother knew she was lying and wouldn't leave it alone. She was trying to save Clara and it got her killed. She watched as her dad beat and raped my mom for days. Then when he put a gun to his own daughter's head, she chose to save herself and stabbed my mother in the heart. How can anyone be so cruel? Why is she allowed to live?"

Logan held me in his arms trying his best to comfort me. When the chief came into his office, Logan motioned for him to leave and give us a little more time. Once he was convinced I was calmed down enough, he left to tell the Chief what I had told him. They immediately gathered a team together to search for Clara's father.

"We are looking for 55 year old Victor Ellis. He is a white male, 5' 10" with brownish grey hair, blue eyes, and a large scar on his left cheek. He is considered armed and dangerous. Proceed with caution, and bring him in any way you can. If you can't shoot to wound, then shoot kill. Be alert and stay safe. No one is to go alone," the chief ordered the officers around.

"If you don't object I would like to stay with Brooke and make some phone calls. We may need some help on this case. No one has seen Mr. Ellis in a couple of years," Uncle David suggested.

"Good idea. We will need to inform the FBI that we are starting our search. I will try and find his last known whereabouts. DO NOT let Brooke out of your site. She is our number one priority at this time."

"I won't go anywhere. I'll stay here and help research

where he might be hiding. I can't help bring him down if I'm dead now can I?"

Uncle David made his phone calls and Logan showed me how to do a few searches on the police database. Over the next few hours we continued our search hitting dead ends every time. When the FBI agents arrived, they took over the search at the station and sent some of their men out into the field.

I paced the room and was starting to give up hope when they got a call that he had been found. They found him at my hotel room and were unable to get a clear shot. One of the agents made contact and he was refusing to come out or talk to anyone but me. Logan said no and at first I agreed with him. That is until I heard he was holding an officer hostage. I agreed to help in any way I could. No one else was going to die because of me. I couldn't live with that.

"This is a bad idea Brooke. You know he just wants to kill you," Uncle David tried to appeal to my scared side.

"I'll be surrounded by the police, S.W.A.T., and the FBI. If he comes out to shoot me, they will kill him first. I need to do this for my parents. Arguing won't get you anywhere."

I turned away from him and looked at the agent who was awaiting my answer. "I will do this under two conditions. First Logan and David must stay here. Second we do this my way. No arguing, and what I say goes. Do you understand me?"

"I can't promise to do it your way, but I will keep the others here. They will be safer and stay out of the way." He looked at Logan and shrugged not knowing how stubborn I really was.

"Then let's go save that hostage. He will not die if I can help it," I suggested with confidence.

When we got to the hotel, a bullet proof vest was put on me and I was handed a phone. I was told to call the room and try to talk him into coming out instead of making things worse. At the very least I had to help get the officer out safely. I nodded in agreement and dialed the number.

"I told you, I'm not talking until Brooke is here."

"This is Brooke you dumbass. Let the officer go or I leave. Your daughter already told me what you did. I already killed her and if given the chance I will kill you too," I lied with conviction.

"I didn't do what she said. You have to believe me," he tried his best to convince me.

"Let the officer go and we'll talk. You already killed my mother and my father. I have nothing left to lose. It would be a pleasure to kill you for them and the torture you inflicted on Clara that turned her into such a vicious monster."

"I'll let the officer go if you come in and talk to me. You have to come in alone. No guns. Any funny business and I'll kill this officer."

"They aren't going to allow that. You know the only way to talk to me is to come out with your hands up, and no weapon. It's the only way."

"That's not an option at this point. You know damn well that they will shoot me as soon as I step out that door. You have to come in here, unless you want this man's blood on your hands."

"Fine, but I'm telling you now, if I come in there, only I will make it out alive. I promise you that." I hung up the phone.

"We can't let you go in there Brooke. It's not safe," the lead agent tried to tell me.

"You don't have a choice. I said we play by my rules. I would rather trade my life for Officer Burke's life. He has a wife and two children. I will not allow them to lose him. This is my decision, not yours. You either let me go in on my own, or you'll have to kill me yourself."

I argued with the FBI agent for over an hour. He kept trying to tell me how dangerous it was. I tried to make him understand that I no longer cared about that. I couldn't let Victor Ellis kill anyone else. It was my decision now, not the FBI's. No one was going to keep me from doing whatever I could to help save Officer Burke's life. Once he realized I was going in with or without their approval he gave in.

"Fine, but you need more than just a vest. Do you know how to use a gun?" he asked.

"No, and I don't need one. I'll throw his out the door after he lets Officer Burke go. Those will be my terms. I want fifteen minutes alone with him before anyone comes in," I demanded.

I walked away from everyone and headed to the hotel room door. I knocked to let him know it was me. "Let the officer leave then as I enter the gun must be tossed out the door. Otherwise I leave."

He agreed to my terms and sent the officer out. As I entered he handed me the gun and I tossed it out before closing us in the room together. I locked the door and turned to face Victor. He looked older than 55. Time had not been good to him and it showed. In my gut, I didn't have the feeling that he was a cold blooded serial killer. I didn't know what to think anymore. I decided not to give in to my gut feeling.

"What do you have to say for yourself? Did you want to gloat about how you killed my mother?"

"I'm trying to tell you that I didn't kill your mother. I admit that I kidnapped her. I will also admit that I slapped her around a bit. I just wanted to scare her enough to stay away. I thought I could scare her and let her go two days later. I tried to explain how Clara really was. Her mother left to try and get Clara some help. Not because I was abusing her."

"What about when you pushed her down the stairs and kicked her in the stomach when she was ten years old?" I challenged.

"She threw herself down the stairs. She was mad because I told her she couldn't have a dog. Her mother was there when it happened. You could ask her if someone hadn't cut the brakes on her car. I'm sure it was Clara that did it. She needs help, and always has."

"So you didn't force her to kill my mom?" I looked at him confused. "How do I know you're telling me the truth? What proof do you have?" I insisted.

"I have a video tape she made," he admitted and placed it in my hand.

"She taped the entire murder. I didn't threaten to hurt you or your fathe and I am truly sorry for what happened. Please call down and tell them they can come get me. I will not run, nor will I fight. I just needed you to know the truth," Victor cried.

I unlocked the door, and called them to let them know it was safe to come up. Moments later, with guns drawn, the FBI entered the room and he willingly allowed them to put him in cuffs. As they escorted him out of the room and into the back of a police car, I handed the tape to Officer Burke. Having already watched the tape, knew what was on it. I headed back outside, and Chief Parks gave me a ride back to the station where I was greeted by Logan with a hug and a kiss.

"Are you okay? Did he hurt you?" He looked me over for any sign that I had been hurt.

"I'm fine. I promise he didn't hurt me. He didn't kill my mother or my father either. Clara killed my mom and taped it and I think she had my father killed trying to frame her dad. I don't know why, but I believe him. If he was a murderer he wouldn't have let me live, nor would he have let them bring him in without a fight."

"If you believe him then so do I. I trust your judgment. Does he have the tape to prove it?"

"Yes, he handed it to me, and I gave it to Officer Burke. He gave it to the FBI agent in charge. I think they are watching it right now."

Logan gave me another hug and I continued to fight back the tears. We all sat around impatiently waiting to see if Victor was telling the truth. An hour seemed like days while we waited for information about what was on the tape. I fidgeted in my seat, and tried not to get up and pace the squad room. It was torture. I almost got up to see what was going on when an agent and Chief Parks came out to speak to us.

"He was telling the truth about the murder. He was nowhere in the room when your mother was killed. He has agreed to stay here in lockup until we find the person Clara hired to frame him. The FBI will take over the investigation for now, but promised that as long as you refrain from attacking Clara again, you can keep on interviewing her. There was also another young girl seen on the tape, but she never shows her face. They are working on finding out who she is," Jackson tried to rationalize.

"Okay, but what will Logan and I do about our safety? He's not healed enough after being shot and I don't feel safe anymore. None of us are safe at this point."

"If I may interrupt, we will have agents all over making sure you're safe. I know you've heard this before, but we will do everything in our power to keep you both safe. We flew Logan's parent's home and are keeping them safe until we finish this case," he explained.

"I guess I will get my stuff from the hotel room and stay at Logan's place if it's safer." I finally gave in. That put a smile on Logan's face.

"No, we need you to stay somewhere they don't know about. Do you know of any new places you could stay?"

"I bought a house, but it has no furniture. I haven't had time. It's been too chaotic."

"Can you order stuff online? I can have two agents pose as the new couple moving in and when it's all set up we will move you in," he suggested.

"I can do that. As soon as we get to Logan's I will order a few items. I will also need to send an agent to the store for food and other items we need."

"We will arrange that as soon as we get things started. For now let's get your stuff and get you over to Logan's place where you can be safer," he agreed.

At the hotel we gathered my belongings and were quickly taken to Logan's apartment. I refused to unpack anything except my laptop and started looking for the needed furniture to get us by. Once it was ordered, I gave the information to one of the agents and got ready for bed. I chose to sleep alone on the couch. I knew my decision upset Logan, but it was what I needed to do at the time. I just hoped he would understand.

Chapter Eleven

It took a couple of days for all the furniture to be delivered. The two agents pretended to be the new couple moving in. They were greeted by neighbors and played the part perfectly. I sent one of them to the store with money and a list of everything we needed. I wanted everything set up and ready for when we moved in.

Walking through the front door of my house, I realized just how bare the house really was. It also needed a lot of work, but at least I knew I would have plenty of time to fix everything the way I liked it. It would be at least a couple of weeks before I could be sneaked out of the house to resume the interviews. Several agents tried to get Clara to talk, but she refused saying she would only speak to me. They told her I moved out of state and wouldn't be able to come back to town for awhile. As far as they knew she believed the lie.

"You know I may go totally insane being stuck in this house for so long. I don't do well as a prisoner. This is not how I imagined moving into my own house would be. Dad was going to help me pick out the perfect furniture and help me paint and fix a few things and then I would move in to my very first home," I sighed in anger and frustration. "Clara has taken everything away from me. I have no happiness left and nothing to look forward to anymore."

Logan looked at me and frowned. "You have nothing

left to look forward to? Do I mean so little to you now? That hurts. If you're so unhappy with me I'll go back to my own apartment and take my chances alone. I won't stay where I'm not wanted," he pouted.

"That's not what I meant and you know it. I lost the last real family I had left and I'm sorry if I can't be all sunshine and roses for you. I'm still trying to process all of the loss. Please don't make it harder on me than it already is. Try to be patient and give me time to heal. I love you, I really do, but I need to be able to say how I feel without you getting mad and making me feel worse. I'm glad you're here." I tried to give him a kiss and he turned away from me. I ran to the bathroom and locked myself in.

I fell asleep on the bathroom floor after several hours of crying and puking. When I came out of the bathroom in the morning Logan was asleep on the floor leaning against the wall next to the bathroom door. I stepped over him and headed to the kitchen to make everyone some breakfast.

"How did things get so messed up?" I thought to myself. "I should have stayed in Kansas City and never come to visit dad."

"You shouldn't think like that," I heard a voice behind me.

"It's true. All I did was cause more hurt and suffering for everyone. I made the mistake of falling in love and now he hates me because I can't deal with all of this. It's too much for any one person to handle and I'm being turned into the bad guy."

"He loves you, trust me. No man will sleep on a hard wood floor next to a bathroom door unless he loves you. He just wants you to let him in. Let him be a part of your grieving. Trust me, he's not going anywhere. Tell him how much you love and appreciate him and show him every day. He blames himself just as much as you blame yourself. I'm a man. I know how we all think," Agent Ben Graves explained.

"You should listen to him," another voice responded. "He's been through a lot with his crazy wife. He knows what he's talking about."

"Are the two of you really married? If not you should know that you're very convincing," I pried.

"Yes we are," they responded in unison.

I finished making breakfast for everyone. I made one big plate to take to Logan for the two of us to share, leaving the agents to fix their own plates. I set the plate on the floor and kissed Logan on the cheek.

"Good morning sweetheart. I made you breakfast," I whispered in his ear.

"Good morning beautiful," he said sitting up and rubbing his neck.

"Why on earth didn't you sleep in the bed you big goober? You shouldn't sleep on this hard floor so soon after surgery."

"I didn't want the first time I slept in it to be without you. I'd rather sleep as close to you as possible," Logan admitted with a smile. "I just want to be a part of your life. If you sleep on the floor, so will I."

"That's just plain silly, you know that?" I picked up the plate and sat next to him on the floor. "Are you hungry? I fixed a plate."

"Where's your food?" he asked with a playful grin.

As he opened his mouth to say something else I put a piece of bacon in it. I laughed as he looked at me confused. He realized he was just going to lose the battle so he might as well give in. He also realized just how hungry he was. We had fought and passed out the night before without even having a chance to have dinner.

In a matter of minutes the plate was empty. I stood up and helped him off the floor. We went to the kitchen to start washing dishes. The agents smiled as we walked in, knowing we had made up.

"Glad to see the two of you smiling again," Kim said with a smile on her own face.

"I think I'll keep him a little longer," I joked.

"Just a little longer? You mean you don't want to keep me forever and ever?" Logan laughed.

"I'd have to think about that. I mean you have a nice body, but not so much in the brains department." I chuckled as he smacked me on the ass with a kitchen towel. "And you're kind of abusive today. Now stand there all sexy and help me do the dishes."

"Yeah well…… okay," he said pulling me into a passionate kiss.

As we washed the dishes, Ben watched curiously and asked, "Why don't you use the dishwasher? It would be faster."

"Because then I couldn't do this..." I scooped up some bubbles and blew them in his direction.

In a matter of minutes the four of us where involved in a bubble and water fight in the kitchen. It lasted a half hour and by the end, we were all soaking wet and sitting on the half flooded floor crying from laughing so hard. It was nice to have a moment of feeling like nothing was wrong. Kim and I grabbed some towels while the men took turns using the shop vac to suck up all the water.

"We totally kicked their asses," I gloated.

"They could never beat us. Not even in their wildest dreams." She giggled as we left the men to finish drying the floor.

"Aren't you guys done sucking yet?" I smirked.

"Nah, that's your job," Logan replied.

"Only in your dreams."

"Well that blows, or doesn't," Logan said confusing himself.

"Stop wasting time or you will ruin my pretty wood floors. Get to work so you can help me pick out paint colors."

"Yes ma'am!" the men exclaimed in unison as they saluted me.

I joined Kim on the couch and we start going over color choices I had previously picked out. We got the colors picked out for the master bathroom before Ben and Logan finally joined us. We all agreed on the colors for the rooms except the living room. None of us could agree on the right colors.

"I'm sorry Logan, but I don't like yellow. I don't want to feel like I am sitting in the center of a lemon meringue pie. I'd be 400 pounds by the end of the year," I admitted.

"Okay no yellow. What about this color?" He held a paint swatch with an ugly shade of green to the wall.

I looked at him puzzled. "Are you smoking crack? That color is disgusting. I was thinking more of a tan color, or a soft brown."

"Whatever color you want honey. It's your house, and you have to be happy with the colors you choose. I'm just glad it's not pink."

"What about purple? Are you okay sleeping in a purple

room?" I kept a serious look on my face the entire time.

"Ummmm…. Okay." He tried not to let on that he hated the idea.

"You're making this too easy. You'll be living here for awhile at least, maybe even longer. I want you to like the colors also."

"As long as I'm here with you, I won't notice the colors. You're all I will ever notice." As he told me this I started to cry again.

I realized, as I gave Kim the paint colors, how many gallons of each, and the money, that Logan was turning me into a mushy mess. I stopped crying and headed up to the bedroom to start moving furniture. I wanted to start painting as soon as Kim returned. I needed to keep myself busy so I wouldn't lose my mind and go stir crazy.

Logan joined me in the room and sat on the bed. He looked depressed and I knew it was because he wasn't able to help me move the big things. However, he did laugh at me while I struggled to move the desk. It was an old, large, antique desk made of solid oak. I struggled for a good fifteen minutes before Logan called for Ben to come help me.

"Why did you try to do this on your own? Are you already losing your mind?" Ben inquired.

"I was trying not to bother you. Can't blame a girl for trying," I shrugged.

"You're not bothering me. Kim and I are happy to help in any way we can. We understand that this isn't easy for either of you. You tell us what colors go where and we will start painting the living room. Once Logan is cleared to be unlazy again, I can help him finish the basement. My dad was a carpenter and I went to work with him in the summers. Just ask and I will help in any way I can," Ben offered.

"Thank you so much. It means a lot to me that you are willing to help. You're right. This isn't easy at all. I'm used to always being on the go. Now I'm stuck in the house and can't leave. I feel so lazy and helpless."

We finished moving the desk and Ben helped me move the bed. By the time we got everything moved Kim returned with all of the paint and supplies. Ben helped bring everything in. I covered the floors and furniture with drop cloths, handed Logan a paint roller, and told him to get to work. Painting was boring and not as much fun as when I was a kid. I remembered painting my room and having a blast. After 20 minutes I took a step back and sighed.

"What's wrong Brooke?" Logan paused.

"It's just not as fun as I remember. When I was a kid I loved painting my room. I did it once a year with my dad." I looked down at my paint brush and sighed again.

"Maybe that's why it's not as fun this time. I can finish painting if you'd like. To give you a break," Logan suggested and continued painting.

I looked down at my paint brush determined to make it fun again. I dipped the brush in paint and while his back is to me I painted a line across his back. He turned around with a smile on his face and painted mine with the roller. We looked at each other, then at the paint, and back to each other, before racing to get more paint. We continued to throw paint at each other before heading back to painting the walls and laughing. Ben and Kim came upstairs to see how far we'd gotten, and burst into laughter seeing the two of us covered in paint.

"Was there a paint explosion up here that we missed?"

Kim asked.

Logan and I looked at each other, smiled, and dipped our brushes in. We started flinging paint at the two of them, and chased them down into the living room where they leveled the playing field. By dinner time we were all covered in paint, and so was the rest of the house. We took turns showering and trying to wash off all of the paint. I uncovered the couch and sat down with a variety of delivery menus.

Once joined by the rest of the group we decided on Chinese food. We watched TV while waiting for the food to arrive. We all froze when a Breaking News story came on. There was another body found in a ditch. The body was tortured and disfigured beyond recognition. All teeth, fingers, and toes were removed making it harder to identify the victim. We looked at each other in horror and jumped when the door bell rang. Ben grabbed his gun and looked out the window to see who it was. He put his gun away when he realized it was only Chief Parks.

"Come in Chief. We just saw the report on the news." Ben welcomed Jackson in.

"What the hell happened here? Are you using paint bombs to paint the walls?" he laughed.

"Nah, just a tiny paint war to make us all smile. It's not easy being stuck inside all of the time. We gotta make our own fun." I smiled waving for him to have a seat. "So what's going on? Do you need something? Are we in more danger? Please say you have good news."

"I'm here to ask a favor. I hate having to ask you this, but we need you to interview Clara again. With the recent body count rising, we need help finding out who her partner was. We've tried to question her and so has the FBI. She's still refusing to talk to anyone but you. If you don't want to see her again, we will understand. You are under no obligation to do this."

"If it will help catch the psychotic murderer still at large, I will do it. I want the sick bastard caught so I can get on with my life. I didn't even get to have a funeral for my father. This has to end and soon."

"Are you sure about this Brooke?" Logan asked.

"I have never been more sure of anything in my entire life. I can't live trapped in my own house anymore. Let's catch this bitch and put an end to the senseless killing sprees." For the first time since my father was killed I was filled with more confidence than ever.

"An officer will pick you up around 10:00am. I'll see you there." Chief Parks smiled as he left the house.

Moments later our food arrived and we sat quietly while we ate. Logan was obviously mad at me. Kim and Ben were confused as to why I would agree to the interview and no one wanted to say anything. After I finished eating I gathered my notebook and a pen. I tried to jot down as many questions as I could think of. I had a feeling she would make me finish hearing about the other murders first, but I was going to try my hardest to get the truth out of her once and for all. No more playing her game. I needed to know the truth. I needed to be free of her and all of her insanity.

By midnight I had given up and decided to try and get some sleep. Everyone else had already gone to bed, but I stayed up trying to figure out the best way to get Clara to talk. I also needed to make sure I could keep my cool. I knew if I attacked her again I would end up getting myself arrested. This was important to me. I had to succeed this time. No more letting her take charge. I had to be in control.

Chapter Twelve

At 6:00am, after a night of tossing and turning, I gave up and got out of bed. I went over my questions some more and added to them. I needed to be ready for anything Clara might throw at me. By 7:00am, I was showered and dressed. I was so tired, but my nervousness would not let me sleep. Last time I encountered her I almost killed her. I almost took her life because of a lie she told me. A lie that, at the time, broke my heart. One that when I found out it was a lie crushed my soul and filled my entire body with a rage unlike any I had ever felt before in my life. I had to keep my wits about me. I couldn't give in to my anger this time. I had to stay strong, and I had to do it for my parents. I was too tired to do much of anything so I chose an old worn out pair of jeans and a comfy t-shirt. I headed back down to the kitchen to make some much needed coffee and go back over my previous notes.

"Why are you up so early?" Logan asked wrapping his arms around me.

"I couldn't sleep so I went over my questions for the day, showered, and now I'm going back over my notes to see what I may have missed," I explained.

"Awwww honey." He leaned in and kissed me. "I missed you taking a shower?"

"Poor baby, you'll get over it. Besides, I am too tired for

your shenanigans this morning."

"You should have awakened me. I would have stayed up with you. Maybe I can help you go over the notes. I've never read them, so maybe fresh eyes will help?"

"Maybe," I replied with a yawn. "Would you like some coffee and some breakfast?" I asked placing a cup of coffee in front of him.

"You're so good to me. Do you want me to help with breakfast? I can make some mean buttered toast."

"No thank you sweetie. I'm going to make French toast, so I think toast is over doing it. Just don't lose your appetite reading those files." I gave him another kiss and started making breakfast.

I finished cooking in time for Kim and Ben to join us in the kitchen. They sat at the island with Logan while I fixed them each a plate and some coffee. Once again we sat quietly while we ate, as if afraid of what the others might say. After breakfast Kim offered to wash the dishes for me so I wouldn't have any added chores.

"Thank you for another delicious breakfast," Ben said handing Kim the dishes.

"Yes, thank you so much. It was wonderful. When this is all over you should open a restaurant. I'd fly out here once a week to eat your cooking." Kim glanced at me with a smile.

"Nah, I only cook for friends and family. I'm glad you like it though." I returned the smile.

"I guess I need to learn how to cook so I can earn my keep around here," Logan joked.

"No way. I am not sharing this amazing kitchen with you. You just have to promise you will always be home for dinner. If work is going to keep you away, you have to call.

No matter what." I filled his coffee cup.

We had just finished going over the files when there was a knock on the door. Ben answered it as I gathered my things. I took a deep breath and was slightly relieved to see Uncle David standing there waiting for me. At least it was someone I knew and trusted.

Kim came down stairs and walked over to us. "I will be in the room with you the entire time."

"Are they afraid I'll try and kill her again? I promise I will be on my best behavior no matter what she says."

"No." She shook her head. "Clara has asked that someone be in the room to protect her. You actually managed to scare a serial killer. I didn't think that was possible, but you did. Don't worry, if you go all ape shit I promise to let you get in a few good punches before I pull you off of her." She put her arm around my shoulder and we left the house.

For once the car ride to the station wasn't quiet. Kim and I went over my game plan, she helped polish up my questions, and we made fun of the guys. They were still stuck at the house while we got to leave for the day. Sure we weren't exactly going to be having fun, but at least we weren't stuck with nothing to do.

A rush of déjà vu swept over me as I entered the station. I was greeted with hugs from worried officers glad to see that I was alive and well. I exchanged a few smiles and paused at the door. It may not have been the first time interviewing Clara, but things had definitely changed over the past weeks. I took a deep breath, opened the door, and headed for my seat at the table. I pulled out my same old recorder and my notebook filled with questions. I pushed record and began the interview.

"Let's get to the reason I'm here. I'm tired of all the lies and want the truth for once in your miserable life. I know you weren't abused. I saw the tape and your father did not force you to kill my mother. So my first question for you is: who is the young girl on the tape?"

"After what you did to me, you don't get to demand anything. I don't know what tape you're talking about. I will not admit to something I didn't do. You won't trap me," she hissed.

"Agent Graves, could you ask them to bring the tape in please?" I asked. "I think we need to refresh her memory."

Kim got up, walked to the door, and poked her head out. "We're ready for the tape now."

They handed her the tape and she put it into the VCR and hit play.

Knowing what was on the tape I turned my head away. I couldn't escape the sound, but at least I could keep from watching it. I focused on Clara and her reaction to watching. A look of anger mixed with fear rushed over her. She turned her head away and begged us to turn it off. I was confused by her reaction. When I heard the other young girl speak, I couldn't remember where, but I knew that voice. I forced myself to look at the video, but didn't recognize her. Kim stopped the tape before I could see anything more than the girl's face. She didn't want to upset me more than I already was. I nodded in her direction as a thank you. It was a relief to know that this time someone had my back.

"Tell me who she is RIGHT NOW!" I yelled and slammed my fists on the table.

"I'm not saying anything until you calm down. If we have a repeat of last time, I will press charges. I will also sue this police department for all the money it has. Are you going to calm down or are am I going back to my cell?" she demanded.

"I'm calm, now answer the question. I want to know who she is," I said as calmly as I possible.

"You already know who she is. If you used your brain to think instead of treating me like crap, she would already be in custody. She's the last person you would ever suspect. That's all I will tell you about her. You can do the rest yourself."

"Why did you set your dad up? What did he ever do to you?" I tried to be calm and attempted to be polite.

"My dad was a bastard. He was always controlling and never let me have any fun. He was one of the strictest parents in the world."

"So you threw yourself down a flight of stairs and hit yourself in the stomach with his boot? All for what? Because he wouldn't get you a puppy to torture?"

"I wasn't going to torture it. I just wanted a friend. My dad wouldn't let anyone come over to the house so everyone thought I was weird. It wasn't fair." Clara acted as though she was going to throw a temper tantrum.

I tried not to laugh at her childish act, but it was too difficult and I let out a small chuckle.

"I'm sorry, but are you still in your terrible two's? Did you ever think that maybe he was afraid of how you treated others? Maybe he wasn't sure if you would have a fit if you were not getting your way and hurt another child?"

"I never hurt anyone else," Clara spat. "I was a good child, and he had no right to tell me no."

"He had every right. It's what parents do. They watch over us and protect us in any way they can. I can't believe I bought your bullshit story and felt sorry for you. You are a worthless piece of shit. Has anything you've ever said to me been the truth? Are you even capable of the truth?" I challenged.

"Everything I have ever said was truth except the story about your mother. I wanted my dad dead and hoped the police would take care of that for me. They never do anything right." She rolled her eyes.

"What happened to your mom? Did you tamper with her car so she wouldn't talk?"

"The bitch was going to ruin everything. She told she was going to the police to tell them about your mother. That weak ass cunt said it was eating her up inside and she just had to tell someone. I couldn't let her ruin my life again so I put a stop to it." She grinned as she recalled what she did to her mother.

"You're a real piece of work. A sick, demented, fuck. You need to tell me who your killing partner is. If you want me to continue with the interviews I need to know I am safe. You tell me or I walk and nobody ever hears your side of the story," I countered.

"I like your style, but we are going to play by my rules or I'll find someone else to tell my story. You finish the interviews and if you survive until the end, I will tell you who she is."

I looked at Kim and she nodded. "I'm going to get some lunch and then let you know what I decide. Enjoy your bread and water."

I turned off the recorder, grabbed my notebook, and we left the room. I rushed into the bathroom and barely made it before throwing up and sobbing uncontrollably.

Kim waited outside the bathroom door letting me have some time to myself. She knew how hard it was for me, but didn't want to make things worse. Moments later I splashed some water on my face and walked outside with Kim.

She looked at me with sadness in her eyes. "I texted Ben to bring us lunch. He and Logan should be here any minute. Let's go inside and wait. I am so sorry you are going through all of this. No one should have to go through so much pain and suffering. I hope you can get your answers." She gave me a big hug.

I felt another set of arms around me and then a bunch more. When I looked up I noticed the entire police department had decided to give me a group hug. It was like some creepy, sappy, scene from a movie, but it made me feel better. My tears turned into laughter and I noticed Ben and Logan walking towards us. They set the food down and came over to join us. I was so overjoyed to feel all the love and support of my friends. Slowly they all went back to work and I gave Logan the biggest hug. I squeezed him so tight he winced at the pain I was causing, but he didn't say a word.

"The four of you can eat in my office. I have to run some errands." Chief Parks pointed towards the direction of his office.

"Thank you. That will be nicer than going back into the interrogation room." We all agreed and sat down to eat.

"You look upset sweetie. What happened? Did she tell you anything helpful?" Logan handed me my food from the diner.

"No, she won't tell me until I finish the interviews about her victims. She denied there was a tape of any kind. I had Kim bring it in so we could show her. I didn't look until right before Kim turned it off, but I did have to listen to all of it. It was awful hearing my mother scream." I looked down at my food unable to eat anything.

"She was a total badass though. She didn't show her

sadness at all. She stared at Clara until the last second. Her look changed to scared and I think she knew who the other girl was on the tape," Kim reassured Logan.

"You know who it is? That's fantastic news babe. Did you tell anyone so they can go get her?" Logan sounded a little too giddy.

"I don't remember who she was. The voice sounded familiar, but I can't remember who it is. I'm so sorry. I want so bad to keep us safe, but I just can't do that. So much has happened recently and I can't remember most of it. If I heard the voice again I would know it, but for now all I'm doing is drawing a blank."

Logan held my chin and looked me in the eyes. "It's okay Hon. Don't force yourself to remember. It just makes things worse. Take your time and relax. We will find her in time."

I leaned in and gave him a kiss. "I love you sweetie. I need to get back to doing the interview so I can make it home in time to make you a nice dinner. We can't keep eating out all of the time. I'll go broke too quickly."

As I got up he smacked me on the ass. "Give her hell Honey. We've got your back."

We got everything set back up and waited for Clara. She was again chained to the floor and table. I turned on the recorder and stared her down. Although it was only minutes it felt like hours before she finally opened her mouth to speak.

Before she could say a word I cut her off. "Let's make this as quick as possible. I don't have time for your bullshit. I just want the truth."

"I'll give you the truth. Let's start with my fourth victim. She was 59 year old Kerry Killman. If I remember correctly, she told me she was from somewhere in Kansas. I saw her at the diner one night and made my plan for how to get her to my place and how to kill her. I walked past the table and stole her friend's phone. Then I headed home to fix up the room just how I needed it. We'll get to that in a bit though. I watched the young man she was with for a few days and figured out his schedule. After I figured out that she was his aunt, and he was safely at work, I texted her from his phone. I told her my car broke down at my friends' house and we needed a ride. It didn't take her long to show up and knock on my door."

I was once again confused. "How did you explain the missing car?"

"That's an easy question. I told her they pushed it back to the barn and that her nephew was in the basement looking for tools. She went down to let him know she was there and I followed close behind. She didn't see him so I pointed to the door to my special room. She opened the door and screamed. I grabbed her head and bashed it into the wall a few times to knock her out. I placed her on the table and strapped her down like the others. This time I had a pulley set up with a rope. I used it to pull up her head and place two spikes underneath it. I made sure they were even with her eyes. I took both phones, turned them off and dropped them into a bowl of left over liquid fire. I watched as they dissolved. I then hid her car in the barn, and went in to sleep."

"What time of day was it? Do you always sleep? Well, when you aren't torturing and killing the innocent?"

"It was late at night on July 18th. You have no idea how tiring it can be to drag people onto that table. Can I continue or do you want to be rude and interrupt me again?" she was clearly agitated.

I rolled my eyes at her in disgust. "Go ahead, even

though you're pretty boring."

"Whatever you say," she continued with her long drawn out explanation. "The next morning after I ate breakfast I went back down stairs. Kerry was awake and in full panic mode. I explained to her the rules of my game. Every time she cried, winced, or screamed I would loosen the rope around her head. I told her the looser the rope the more she had to work at keeping her own head up. It was fun to see the fear in her eyes when she realized there were spikes under her head. It made me smile, and I fought to hold in a laugh. I grabbed a cigar cutter from my drawer of toys. I was surprised when she didn't make a sound. She even kept her eyes fixed on mine. I think the fat bitch thought I would free her if she pretended to be strong. I removed her hideous wedding ring, placed her finger in the cigar cutter, and chopped it off. She tried so hard to stay silent, but she let out a scream. I know it hurt, but she knew the rules, so I loosened the rope a little bit. I placed another finger in the cutter and she winced. So I loosened the rope again. The force of her head falling wouldn't be enough for what I had planned, but she didn't realize that. I put the cigar cutter back in the drawer, and pulled out a knife. I used it to push her shirt up, then started carving random symbols and words into her stomach. I stopped when I noticed her crying, and once again loosened the rope. I told her that if she broke the rules one more time she would have to hold her head up all on her own."

"How were you going to get those spikes to go through her skull? It's not an easy task."

"First of all, the spikes were made of solid steel. Second she was also being held up by another device. I invented it myself. It was strapped to her just right so that when she couldn't hold her head up any longer and it started to drop, she would be pulled down onto the spikes at around fifty miles per hour. Pretty clever, right?" she smiled at her own cleverness.

"If you say so," I replied sickened by her fascination with torture and murder.

"It's art to me. You wouldn't understand."

I could tell by her tone that I had struck a nerve. Clara both pissed me off and amused me. I knew it was odd to feel amused by anything she said or did, but she was intriguing at times. I was curious about why she murdered innocent people. I even had doubts about things she told me.

"That's not even close to art. You're a sick fuck. I don't know how you sleep at night."

"I sleep just fine at night, thank you very much," she admitted. "I took a break and ate some lunch. I needed to think of one last way to torture her. I wanted to make it good and decided the best thing to do while I finished eating. I washed the dishes and headed back down. I grabbed a metal bat and used it to bash her in the knees repeatedly, laughing as I heard the bones shatter. Kerry screamed out in pain once more so I removed the rope from around her head. I sat in a chair and watched as she struggled to hold her head up. She was one strong mother fucker. I figured it would be a matter of minutes, but it took much longer than that. In fact, I fell asleep waiting I was so bored. Imagine my surprise when I woke up, about 4 hours later, just in time to see her head pulled down with such force that the spikes went through her skull and right through her eye sockets. Her eyes were stuck to the tip of the spikes. Blood splattered onto the ceiling, all over her face and clothes, and even over to my chair. I expected it to kill her and was pleasantly surprised to hear that she was still screaming. I quickly left the room to clean all of the blood off of me. After I cleaned up, I met a friend for a late night dinner. We ate and talked for an hour before I went back home to check and see if the bitch was finally dead, or if I needed to think of something else."

I tried to stay calm and not react to what Clara was saying. "You seem to be a little over dramatic when killing people. Was she dead or did you fail again?"

"She wasn't dead yet. I found an old needle from my grandma's diabetes supply, filled it with bleach and injected it into her vein. I filled the syringe with more bleach and injected it into her heart for good measure. In a matter of minutes, she was dead. I left her there until the next night when it was safe to dump her body. Do you want my next victim or do you have somewhere you need to be?"

"Whatever, I'm leaving. You can rot in hell for all I care. Go choke on a maggot." I quickly gathered my items and left.

"Don't let her get to you like that Brooke. She's not worth it. Let's go home and try to relax. The men can figure out how to cook us dinner." Kim put her arm around me and we had an officer drive us home.

When we walked into the house, both men were sitting on the couch drinking beers, covered in paint. We smiled and decided we should fix dinner after all. They met us in the kitchen and we talked about our day while preparing steaks, baked potatoes, and green beans.

"How was your day?" I asked Logan before pulling him into kiss.

"It was pretty good. We finished painting the living room, our bedroom, and did the master bathroom. Then we sat and had a beer or two. How was your day?" he smiled at me lovingly.

"It sucked as usual. I had to listen to another horrible

story about torture and murder. She still isn't saying anything about her partner. She describes everything as if she did it all alone. I don't think she's strong enough to lift any of those bodies by herself. Tomorrow I will listen to the last two victims. Then, hopefully, I can get her to tell me who her partner was. In the meantime, I brought home the video so I can try to remember who the other girl is. I know that voice. I know it won't be easy, but I have to try and figure this out." I turned back around to check the steaks.

Ben looked at me and frowned. "I don't think that's a good idea. We will find out who she is, and arrest her. Please don't put yourself through this. You're already losing sleep. If you're too upset you might end up killing her this time."

As I portioned out dinner and handed everyone their plate I tried to explain why I wanted do this.

"I promised my father I would find out the truth about Mom. Now he's dead too. I can't have him looking down on me full of disappointment. Unless this happens to you, you will never understand the importance. If I stop trying to find the truth the bad guys win. I will not allow them that satisfaction. This is my journey to go on and I know that no matter how challenging it may be, I can do this. I *will* do this."

Logan put a piece of steak in my mouth after realizing I wasn't eating dinner. "First you need to eat. Then I will watch the tape with you. I refuse to let you go through this alone. You have a support system and we want to help you. Now eat all your dinner or you won't get any pie later."

I ate as much as I could handle at the time.

Before I even got up Kim had cleared the table and started on the dishes. I tried to help her, but she refused my help. I went upstairs to see how the bedroom turned out and if they did the bathroom properly. I was surprised to see Ben and Logan putting all of the furniture back where it belonged. When I walked into the bathroom I noticed they swapped the colors. The wall and trim colors were the right colors, but not the way I wanted it. I was however, pleasantly surprised to see that it looked better than what I planned.

"Sorry we painted the walls the trim color and the trim the wall colors. We didn't realize it until we were finished. We will fix it for you tomorrow," Logan offered.

I looked up at him and smiled. "It's perfect. I like this a lot better than what I was going to do. Are you sure that you and Ben are straight? You two could be interior decorators."

"I am so not gay. I'm not sure about Ben though. I think he was staring at my ass today," he replied and shot Ben an odd look over his shoulder.

Ben joined us in the bathroom and smacked Logan on the ass. "I bat for both teams big boy. If things don't work out for you and Brooke, my wife and I would take you in."

I couldn't tell if he was serious or not, so I just dropped it. It was hard enough being jealous of all the women who stared at him. I didn't need to think about men trying to steal my man too. Kim joined us and just shook her head at Ben. After staring at the walls a few more minutes we went to the living room to start watching the tape. Logan made sure the curtains were closed tight while Ben hooked the VCR up to the TV. I put in the tape and pressed play. I snuggled up to Logan and tried to convince myself it was nothing more than a bad horror movie. I had to turn my head away several times and Logan would let me know when the other girl was on the screen. I watched the video a few times before I had to run to the bathroom and throw up.

I sat on the floor and cried. I couldn't figure out who she was and I felt like big failure. That night I skipped dessert and went straight to bed. Even though my dreams were all about seeing my mom murdered, I slept through the night.

Chapter Thirteen

I woke the next morning too depressed to interview a psychotic, murdering bitch. I got up and got ready to go anyway. I had to fight the feelings and put on my big girl panties. This needed to be over with as soon as possible. I decided not to take a lunch break so I could try and get the last two victims over with. I couldn't handle too many more days of listening to Clara gloat about her killings. It was starting to take a toll on my psyche.

I packed a lunch for myself and as I got ready to pack one for Kim, Ben informed me that she was sick and he would sit in on the interview with me. I offered to make him lunch, but he said he didn't need one. I grabbed a few cans of soda, filled my cup with coffee, and we headed out the door. I felt bad for not waking Logan up to say goodbye, but I knew he needed more sleep. He spent too many nights sitting up with me and keeping me company, or sleeping on hardwood floors because I threw a fit, and I knew I would see him later. At least I left him a note telling him how much I loved him. It was better than nothing.

I sat in the room and got ready like I always did. Something didn't feel right to me and my gut was telling me to get up and walk out. I ignored it and tried to relax. I looked at Ben who had the same gut feeling. Chief Parks entered the room and sat across the table from me with a sad look on his face.

"We just got a call from Kim," he tried to explain but I stopped him.

"Is Logan alright? What's wrong? I can't lose anyone else." I got up and paced the room in full panic mode.

"He's ok for now, but…" I stopped him again.

"What do you mean 'for now'?" I shouted a little too loudly causing both men to jump slightly.

"Stop interrupting me, and let me finish," the chief demanded. I sat back down and let him continue.

"Someone made it into the house while Logan and Kim were sleeping. A briefcase was put in each room, and handcuffed to Logan and Kim. The bomb squad is on scene and they are working as fast and as carefully as possible to remove the bombs. We can't take you there in case the person responsible is hiding and watching. I will not put your life in any more danger. We are prepared to send an officer down to tell Clara you didn't come in today. That is your choice."

"No," I said with confidence. "Bring her up. The sooner I get this part done, the sooner I find out who is doing all of this. I need to do this. Please send in another officer so Ben can go to the scene. He should be there when Kim walks out of the house alive."

Ben shook his head at me. "I'm not leaving. I want to know who this is just as much as you do. It's personal now. I will help you through this."

"Thank you Ben. This means a lot to me." I grabbed his hand and squeezed it to show my support. "Please send Clara up. Ben and I will get to the bottom of this."

Minutes later they brought Clara into the room followed by her lawyer. He greeted me and shook my hand.

"You brought your lawyer today. Are you feeling a little

scared?" I inquired.

"I'm here to advise my client to tell you who her partner was. I have told her that additional charges are being filed since she is not willing to cooperate and more people are dying or are in harm's way. She told me she wanted to file charges against you for attempted murder, but I explained that it would be a very bad idea. I want her to help as much as possible," he explained with sympathy.

"Let me guess. Clara wants a plea bargain for giving up her partner?" Ben countered.

"She does, but I know at this point it's no longer an option. She knows that she should have been forthcoming with important information from the beginning."

"Are you ready to be honest and tell us the truth Clara? We may be able to take the death penalty off the table if you help us out," Ben disclosed trying to further tempt her to tell us the truth.

"I will take whatever punishment. I will be honest and tell you what I know, but I have to start from the beginning. I must also tell you that the main reason I am doing this for you is due to death threats she has been sending me. Her name is Echo Shay. I met Echo when I was visiting my grandparents as a young child." I stopped her and looked at Ben.

"I'm sorry Clara. I promise I will be right back and listen to your entire story. I will also listen to what you say about the other two victims. I need to tell the chief her name so they can start the search." I smiled and quickly left the room.

"I understand. I hope they find her. She is killing the wrong people."

I ran into the chief's office and interrupted his meeting

with a couple of the FBI agents. "I'm sorry to barge in like this. I know why the young girl's voice was familiar. I interviewed her right after the press conference. It's the woman who found the bodies, Echo Shay. Clara just told me her name, and it all came together. She found the bodies in the middle of a field? She found the bodies in the middle of a field that wasn't even hers? She must have had a fight with Clara and set her up to take the fall. I'm not sure where she fits in on the murders, but I know she does somehow. Maybe she helped move all of the bodies, or even helped kill the victims. I will find out, but I had to let you know."

The chief excused himself from the room, and walked me back to the interrogation room. "We just found the body of a woman fitting Echo's description 2 miles from your home. We won't know anything until an autopsy is done. I will let you know as soon as I have the answers."

"Thank you and I hope it is her. I just want this to be over." I went back in and whispered the information to Ben.

"I'm sorry. Clara, please continue."

Although still afraid for Logan and Kim I was partially relieved that after this was over, we might be able to return to normal.

"You look happy? Do they know where she is already?" Clara asked sounding excited.

"I'll explain later. Please continue with your story."

"Like I said, I met Echo when I was young. We were a lot alike. We ate the same foods, had the same toys, and loved the same music. We were best friends. She was younger than me, but that didn't matter. We played in the fields on nice days and sat inside playing games when it was raining too hard or too cold to be outside. For an entire summer we did everything together. We even had the chickenpox together. My grandma let her stay at our house while her parents worked and when we were both sick. She loved taking care of us. When school started we both threw fits because we were in different grades and couldn't be in the same class together. When not in school we spent as much time together hanging out as we could. We hardly ever got in any trouble." She paused as she remembered a nicer life.

"What started the trouble for the two of you? Did something bad happen?" Ben asked trying to help move things along.

"I'm getting to that. When I was 10, all of the kids at school made fun of me for hanging out with a 7 year old. It made me so mad that I started fighting my classmates. I was in one fight a month to start. By high school I was getting into fights on a daily basis. If I wasn't at school and fighting, I was skipping. I didn't make friends easily, and was very protective of Echo. Isn't everyone protective of their best friend? By the time I was seventeen, we were both in to drugs and alcohol. My father and I fought all the time and my mother ended up in rehab. Echo and I watched the movie Fight Club one night while we were high on one of the many drugs we did. We thought it was awesome and went into the basement to have our own little fight club. We beat the hell out of each other. There was blood everywhere. We were covered in bruises and I think I broke her nose. The next day my father saw us and went ballistic. He told Echo that she was no longer welcome in his home and grounded me until my 18th birthday. Echo knew she couldn't go home all beaten up without an explanation and we were both so pissed off at my father, that we made a plan to get back at him. She was supposed to go to the police and say my father beat and raped her."

"Did she go to the police, or did she back out?" I asked.

"She did go to the police, and they investigated my father. They found no evidence of him ever hitting anyone. He had no cuts, bruises, or anything. We didn't think the plan through. I went to the police myself to tell them my story. That's when I saw your mother and she had to try to fix everything. She just couldn't leave it alone. She brought DFS to the house. After investigating they did nothing. It pissed my dad off that she was butting her nose in other people's business. So he kidnapped her in hopes of scaring her enough to drop it. On the last day, Echo talked me into torturing her so my dad would go to prison. I said no at first, but after hours of hearing her tell me how awesome it would be to get rid of my dad, I finally agreed. She said we were only going to hurt your mom a bit. As you saw, it didn't turn out that way. That was the first time I tortured and killed anyone. I am sorry I took your mother from you. I am not, however, sorry about killing the others."

"Do you want me to forgive you or something?" I questioned. "Because that will never happen. You should have thought of that before you tortured and killed my mom. You took her from me and from my father. He never got over it, and died before I could find out the truth," I shouted. I looked away from her while fighting back tears of anger. "I think I'm done for the day. I need to go find out if Logan is going to be okay or not. I'll finish the interview later." I grabbed my stuff and left the room.

I rushed outside to get some fresh air and I ran right into Logan. I wrapped my arms around him and pulled him close. I was so thankful he was alive and unharmed. My fear, anger, and sadness all drained away as I held on to him. I didn't want to let go but he forced my arms off of him and went inside. I walked in behind him saddened that he didn't even talk to me. He was led into one room, Kim into another, and the officer who was supposed to be at the front door was taken into the chief's office. I froze not knowing or understanding what was going on. No one said a word to me so I found an empty seat and sat. Ben joined me with the same look of confusion.

"Did they do something wrong?" I asked Ben with concern in my eyes.

He looked at me knowing something was wrong. "I have no idea. How could they be in trouble for something they didn't do?"

"Just when I think my life might get back to normal, another bomb is dropped on my happiness." I fought back more tears. "Wait, you don't think they are trying to pin Echo's murder on one of them do you? They didn't even know she had anything to do with this. As far as Logan is concerned she was just some woman who happened to find the bodies and who I interviewed. Please tell me this is all a dream. I can't handle any more."

"How could they think either of them would do such a thing? They know better," he tried to assure me.

"Maybe they just want to get their stories about what happened?"

"I really hope so."

We spent the next two hours not talking or even looking at each other. I ran through a million and one reasons why all of this was happening, but I had no answers. All I could do was sit and wait. It felt like years had passed when Logan finally exited the room. He sat at his old desk and wouldn't even look at me. I walked over to him and he turned his head away from me.

"What did I do wrong now?" I demanded.

"I'm sorry, but I can't do this anymore. I love you and I thought I could handle it, but I was almost blown up today. It's too much, and I'm not living my life in fear anymore.

I'm going to go stay with my parents until I find a place of my own. They already put in a transfer to the police department there." He started packing his personal things.

"So, were you just planning on leaving without telling me? Did you ever plan on talking to me at all?" I yelled causing everyone to look up at us.

"You're making a scene. Can we talk later while I'm packing?" he sounded annoyed.

"No we can't. You also can't go into my house anymore. I'll pack your shit and leave it in the yard for you. After that you can forget my name and number. You're just like the rest of the worthless men on this planet. Not one of you is worth the oxygen you breathe." I slapped Logan across the face and turned away from him. Ignoring the fact that Echo might still be alive and waiting to kill me, I started walking home.

Ben ran out of the station after me yelling. "You can't go home on your own. You know it's not safe."

I turned around and yelled back at him. "It doesn't matter anymore. Let the bitch kill me. At least then I could relax."

I continued walking home silently praying that someone would kill me, when I heard a loud bang and felt a sharp pain in my back. Before passing out I heard people screaming, and saw a familiar face.

I woke up two months later in a dark, cold hospital room. I had an IV in one arm, and a breathing tube down my throat. It sent me into full panic attack setting off all of the alarms. Several nurses rushed in to check on me and make sure everything was alright. A nurse rushed out of the room and back very quickly. In a matter of minutes I was asleep again.

When I woke up again the tube had been removed and Uncle David was sitting next to my bed. I turned my head away from him trying to remember what happened.

"I'm glad you're awake," he said with a smile. "I was afraid you would sleep forever. The whole town is worried about you."

I turned to face him, but couldn't manage to force a smile. "What happened to me? How long ago did it happen? I'm so confused right now. Please explain everything to me."

"You were shot in the back two months ago. We believe it was Echo who did it, but we still haven't found her. We think she escaped during all of the chaos," he tried to clarify.

"I thought Echo was dead. How does a dead woman shoot me?" I looked at David hoping for some kind of answers.

A familiar voice responded. "The body they found dead was not Echo. It turns out she had an identical twin sister. If it hadn't been for finger prints and dental records we never would have known." I looked toward the door and there stood Logan.

David stood up and walked towards the door. "I'll let the two of you talk."

"What do you want Logan? You left me, remember? You forfeited all your rights to care about what happens to me. I suggest you leave, because I don't want to hear anything you have to say. I will have you arrested."

It had been two months since he broke my heart, but due to my coma it was the last thing I truly remembered. The wound he caused was still too fresh and the sight of him made me sick to my stomach. I still loved him, but I was nowhere near ready to forgive him.

"You have to let me explain. It was not my choice to leave. I figured if I lied to you it would make things easier. I also knew that if I had told you the FBI wanted us to separate until all of this was over that you would stop helping and they probably wouldn't have found Echo until after you were dead."

"Echo was already dead though. At least that's what they thought."

"One of the officers knew Echo from a time she was arrested at 18. Echo had a tattoo on her neck, and this girl didn't. We decided it was better to make her think that we thought she was dead. We hoped she would make a mistake so we could catch her. It was all part of the plan."

"Why wasn't I told about the plan? Did no one think I was smart enough to handle it? I blame you for my being here. You agreed to lie to me and rip my heart out. I may never forgive you for your part in this."

"They needed it to be as real as possible. If people saw that I was gone and you were out alone in public, word would get around and Echo could slip up."

"So I was going to be out there on my own to get shot? Their plan worked wonders. Now I'm stuck in this damn hospital bed." I turned my head away from him disgusted at the thought.

"There's more I need to tell you." Logan stared at the floor. "Besides a couple of nurses, the doctor, the FBI, and a couple of officers, everyone thinks you are dead."

"They think I'm what?" I shouted.

"Shhhhh. You can't yell. As soon as the doctor says you can leave, Kim will come give you a new look."

"What about my house, my money, and all of my

belongings?"

"A fake will was forged by the FBI leaving everything to me. All of the money is still there and I've been staying at your house. When all of this is over everything will be transferred back to you. We are working as hard as possible to find her and get you back to the normal life you deserve."

"I don't want to be a prisoner again. I just want a normal life like everyone else. Isn't there anything else they can do?" I pleaded.

"This is the only way to keep you safe for the time being. I promise this time we will keep you safe from all harm. I'll go get the doctor so he can make sure you are doing okay." He turned and left the room.

I had a few minutes to think about everything while I was alone. I decided to play along for a little while, but I was not going to make it easy on any of them. The doctor did a check-up and said I could go home the next day as long as everything remained the same by morning. The next morning, since I was still doing well, I was released. They sneaked me into my own house and Kim chopped and colored my hair. I wasn't happy, but I had no control over my own life anymore. I was to do whatever they told me to do. It was like once again being in my own personal hell. I sat on the couch watching movies and trying to ignore everyone for the entire day. I refused to eat anything they set in front of me. I knew it was childish, but it was the only way to get my point across.

"Stop acting like a child Brooke," Logan spat at me.

"Stop telling me what to do," I replied. "You have no say in any part of my life from now on. I will never forgive you for going along with the FBI or for breaking my heart."

"I told you I didn't have much of a choice. We were

running out of options very quickly," he explained while trying to stay calm.

"Logan, did you tell her everything? Does she know about the video they found at the scene?" Ben inquired.

"No he didn't," I said confused. "What video are they talking about? Stop keeping information from me."

"I didn't want her to get upset. She would have just blamed herself again," he admitted.

"Blame myself for what? What was on that video? Someone better start talking," I demanded.

"If you won't tell her I will." Kim stared at Logan.

"Fine, but can you give us a few minutes please? I want to be alone when I tell her." He waved them out of the room. "The video was of my ex girlfriend. Apparently since I had been ignoring her phone calls and messages, she decided to come see me."

"Why were you ignoring her? Is that how you treat all of your exes?" I said condescendingly.

"I don't treat them all like that. Only her, and with good reason. I only dated her a few months and when I found out she had been cheating on me for the last month, I broke up with her. I promised myself it was the last time I would ever speak to her. I eventually had her number blocked so she could no longer contact me. That's why she came to town."

"Who sent the video and what happened on it?"

"The video was taken and sent by Echo. She is clearly seen brutally torturing and eventually killing my ex. It wasn't just my ex though. She was very pregnant." He started to cry and I gave in, wrapping my arms around him. "She must have been 7 or 8 months pregnant. Echo cut the baby out of my ex right before finishing her off. The video cut off after that. After a month of searching, the body was found, but there were no remains of any newborn baby."

"That's awful, and I am so sorry you had to go through it. Are they still looking?" I tried to comfort him.

"They are still looking. The FBI found proof that a new born was brought in to a hospital 45 minutes from here on the day the video was taken. The woman explained that she had given birth at home and wanted to make sure her baby was okay. She refused an exam on herself and said she only needed her baby checked. They didn't like the idea, but checked the baby over. The woman they described was Echo, but with different colored hair. The baby was early, but given a clean bill of health and sent home. Because they did all of the blood work, it was on file at the hospital. We are still trying to determine if I am the father or not. I never knew who she cheated on me with, so that's a dead end. It scares me to know that I could not only be a father, but that some sick psychopath might have her."

"It's a girl? They will find her. I know they will. You have to keep thinking positive. Trust me, I know how hard it is, but it's the only thing that will get you through this. I'm sorry I was so hateful to you. If I had known..." I tried to say but he cut me off.

"You had every right to be angry. What I did was unforgivable. I only kept the information from you because I knew you were already blaming yourself for everything that happened. This is not your fault. None of it is. Can we just start over again? I don't want you mad at me anymore. I already had to see my ex murdered, what could be my child cut out of her, and you in a coma after being shot. I don't think I can handle you being mad at me."

I reached out my hand to him. "Hello. My name is Brooke Stevens. It's a pleasure to meet you." We both broke out into laughter.

I finally gave in and ate something while we all sat in the living room watching a movie. After I ate, I snuggled up to Logan and fell asleep in his arms. When I woke up in the morning I was no longer on the couch. Instead I was snuggled next to Logan in bed. I smiled and watched him sleep. It felt good to be back at home and in my own bed. It felt even better to have him so close to me again. I laid my head back down on his chest and just listened to his heart beat.

"Good morning beautiful," he said, and kissed the top of my head.

"Good morning sexy." I replied rolling over and stretching out.

I looked over at Logan, smiled, got up, and started stripping off my clothes as I walked to the bathroom. I started the shower and got in without closing the bathroom door. As I let the hot water run over my body, Logan peeked through the shower curtain. I smiled and pulled him in, still half dressed. We locked lips in a passionate kiss as I struggled to remove the rest of his now wet clothes. We spent the next hour going from the shower to the bed and becoming one with each other before heading down to eat a late breakfast.

"Sounds like someone made up this morning." Kim laughed.

I turned my head and blushed, trying not to make eye contact with anyone at the table.

"Maybe just a little."

"It sounded like more than just a little. You used up all the hot water too." Ben laughed so hard it made him snort.

"My bad!" I exclaimed. "Guess we need a better water heater. Since I'm broke and dead now someone else will have to pay for it." I looked over at Logan and smiled.

"I'm guessing you mean me?" he asked. "We should get a tankless water heater. Then as long as the power doesn't go out we will always have hot water. We'll take care of that later. Right now I need to get ready for work, since someone made me late."

I fixed Logan lunch to take with him as he went up and got ready. When he came back down I handed it to him and gave him a kiss. I was a little sad to see him leave for the day. I spent the rest of the day cleaning up, finding busy work, and researching tankless water heaters. I knew that either my house would be the cleanest in town or I'd go completely crazy if this kept up. How was I going to handle being stuck in the house for so long, especially with the holidays coming up so soon? I had to find a way to get out of the house and I didn't mean just sitting on the back porch. I had to come up with a plan.

Chapter Fourteen

It took two weeks before they let me go out in public with my new look. I was closely watched and it was only the grocery store, but damn it felt nice to finally leave my house. I picked up everything needed for a nice Thanksgiving dinner. Uncle David and Aunt Elizabeth agreed to spend the holiday with us so I would feel like I had family with me. I offered to make everything except the desserts. That was being done by Aunt Elizabeth. When I returned home and got all of the groceries put away, I sat down and finalized our Thanksgiving menu. I made sure I had everything needed. I had three days to finish plans and get any prep work done.

I woke up early on Thanksgiving morning to make breakfast and start on our big meal of the day. I felt bad that Kim and Ben had to be away from their families, so I insisted that they spend the day relaxing. Logan worked a short shift then came home to help me with cooking. He was a horrible cook so he was in charge of peeling and cutting the potatoes, soaking and breaking fresh green beans, and opening cans.

"Come on. Why won't you let me help cook anything?" Logan whined.

"Your greatest talent in the kitchen is burning water. I want dinner to be edible, not burnt to a crisp," I teased playfully.

"I only ruined one pan, and if I remember correctly you're the one who distracted me. I did not lure myself up stairs, so that one was on you," he smirked.

"You're the one who left the burner on. You had plenty of time to turn it off. Therefore it is still your fault." We burst out laughing and were joined by both Kim and Ben.

"What are we laughing about?" Ben asked.

"Logan is a pro at burning water and blaming others for it." I looked over and winked at Logan.

Kim started laughing and almost fell off of her stool. "You're both to blame for that one. Neither is so innocent."

"Can someone fix me a glass of wine please?" I asked as I fanned myself. "I also need a window opened. It's too hot in here."

Kim poured a glass of wine while Ben opened a window. Logan tried to give me the sad puppy dog look, so I told him he could make the green bean casserole. I figured as long as he could follow directions it should be safe.

I was so glad I had two ovens in my house. It made cooking such a big meal easier. An hour before dinner was finished, Uncle David and Aunt Elizabeth arrived with four different pies. I joined the others as we sat around talking and waiting for the turkey to finish cooking. I could tell something was wrong by the look on Uncle David's face, but I didn't press him for information. I wanted my first holiday without my father to be a good one.

We finally finished eating and the men took over putting away leftovers and cleaning up the mess. Kim, Elizabeth, and I sat on the couch talking and trying to ignore the game that was still on. After about an hour the men joined us in the living room and we all discussed future plans.

"So when do I get to do more than just go to the grocery

store? You know this is driving me nuts right?" I stuck out my bottom lip and pouted.

"As soon as we know it's safe for you out there. I refuse to let you be in harm's way," Logan answered sincerely.

"Are you even close to finding Echo? If not just put me in a crowded place, paint a target on me, and be sure you take her down before she takes me down," I said half joking.

Everyone turned to me and stared in disbelief. I tried to pass it off as bad joke, but I could tell it wasn't working. I tried to change the subject, but no one seemed to be in the mood to talk anymore. David pulled Logan aside and they whispered back and forth. As I approached them they stopped whispering and looked at me like I was intruding. Logan had tears in his eyes and I knew something bad had happened.

"Logan, sweetie, what's wrong? " I wrapped my arms around him.

"I'll let David tell you. So you know I don't agree with him at all. I'm going up to bed. I'll see you later." He kissed me and stormed off.

"What is he talking about David? What did you say to make him so upset?"

"I told him that the FBI wants you back in and questioning Clara. They want all of the information you can get from her and they want you to start in two days. I am against this also. If you come out of hiding and people know you're alive, it will no longer be safe for you. I urge you to say no. They can't force you to do anything," he did his best to convince me.

"I'll think about it and won't make a hasty decision. I promise to take all the time I can." I hugged Uncle David and said goodnight to everyone.

After I said goodbye to those leaving, I headed upstairs to get ready for bed. Logan was already in bed with a card sitting next him. I closed the bedroom door, changed into my nightgown, and sat on the bed so I could read the card. The card was so beautiful it brought tears to my eyes. I leaned over and kissed Logan, but he stopped me and smiled. He pulled out a small purple box and handed it to me without saying a word.

As I opened the box with a confused look on my face he sat up and looked me in the eyes, "Brooke Stevens, I have loved you from the first time I laid eyes on you. When you walked up to me, my heart skipped several beats. I have never loved anyone as kind, caring, strong, and independent as you. I would be the happiest man on earth if you would agree to be my wife. I promise to always let you be who you are and never try to change any part of you."

"Oh, Logan!" I cried and wrapped my arms tight around him. "I want nothing more than to marry you. I promise the only thing I will ever change about you is your inability to cook. You must learn the basics."

Logan placed the ring on my finger and pulled me into the sweetest, most passionate kiss of my entire life. We didn't get much sleep that night. Instead we went back and forth between making wedding plans, and making love. Neither of us wanted to get up the next morning, but Logan had to work, and I had a decision to make.

We settled on cereal for breakfast and I was sitting alone at the island drinking coffee. Kim came down and joined me. I showed her my ring and we gushed over it for an hour before Ben finally made it downstairs. I bragged about the proposal for another hour, before someone else decided to change the conversation.

Ben explained why he was late coming down. "The boss called again. He wants me to talk you into doing the interviews Brooke. I tried to explain that it was bad idea, but he is adamant about you doing this. He says Clara knows where Echo is and isn't talking. I still say it's the worst idea ever. I can't in good conscience try to talk you into something so dangerous. Please don't do it."

"I agree with you Ben. It's a very, very bad idea for me. I also know that it needs to be done. I'm so torn about this. I don't want Logan upset with me, nor do I want to risk getting shot again. I do however want and need more answers. If nothing else, maybe I can help find that poor missing baby. It's killing Logan that he may have a child out there who is stuck with a murderer. I don't know what I'm going to do. Is there somewhere safer they can take Logan and I if I decide to do it? I need a 100% guarantee of our safety or I will never do it. I also need to make sure Logan won't leave me if I do."

"I know Logan will be mad, probably even furious, but I don't think he will ever leave you for doing what you think is right. No matter how stupid it is," Kim teased.

"Very funny Kim." I faked a laugh. "Ben, I think I picked out the tankless water heater to get. Will you look at it for me please? If it's the right one I'll order it today. Logan already has too much on his mind."

"Sure thing kid," he joked around. "Just bring up the link on your computer and I'll take a look after I eat something."

I pulled up the link for Ben and started cleaning the house. I tried so hard to distract myself so I wouldn't think about what I was being asked to do. I only stopped once to eat lunch and order the water heater, and then again to have dinner ready when Logan got home. While preparing dinner I started thinking about my options. Should I risk my life again to help the FBI, or should I tell them where to shove it? Could they really protect me this time? I was so distracted that I sliced my finger with the knife.

"Son of a fucking bitch!" I screamed causing Kim to run into the kitchen.

Wrapping my finger in a towel she yelled for Ben. "Honey, I need you to come turn everything off in the kitchen while I take Brooke to see if she needs stitches."

Ben ran in the kitchen as Kim grabbed our coats and purses and led me out to the car. Two hours and five stitches later we were finally able to leave. We arrived at the house to a wonderful meal cooked by Ben, and a very worried Logan pacing the living room. I smiled at Logan and held up my hand while giggling to let the men know I was okay.

Logan ran over to me and wrapped his arms around me. "I was so worried about you."

"It's just a few stitches. I promise I'll live," I assured him.

"How did this happen? Where you doing knife tricks or something?" he said without taking a breath.

"No!" I laughed. "I was just a little distracted. I didn't cut my hand off or anything. You gotta lighten up babe. While you are very cute when you go into panic mode, it's not very sexy."

"I'm sorry. Ben only said you went to the emergency room. He didn't fully explain why. I can't help but worry about you. I don't think I could ever go through what I did a couple months ago and survive. It scared me so much, and I still feel guilty." He pulled me in for another kiss.

"I know Logan. I get that you feel bad, but you didn't make me run out of there on my own and act like a damn child," I reassured him. "Now let's go see if the food tastes as good as it smells. Maybe we will get lucky and not all have food poisoning."

"That's not funny you know. I happen to be a wonderful chef. Kim is the one who causes food poisoning," Ben retorted.

Kim threw her napkin at Ben with a frown. "I'm not that bad. I can make pancakes as long as I have Bisquick."

"Guess we all need to talk about a few things. We all know what they want me to do. Also we're all in total agreement that it's a very bad idea. I want to discuss this though. It's not something I can make a rush decision on, but I have to give an answer tomorrow. I need help with this."

"Let me tell you what happened at the station today, then we can discuss what decision you want to make," Logan suggested. "One of the officers has been allowing Clara to have private visitors. A young man has been bringing her notes, and taking notes back to Echo. We are keeping quiet and pretending we don't know right now. Today we had him followed. He dropped a piece of paper in a flower pot, and sure enough Echo came by and picked it up."

"Is she in custody? Please tell me I can live my life again!" I exclaimed hoping I was right.

"I'm sorry Hon. They lost track of her and she got away. They will try again next time. In light of this new information and promises of extra security, I think it might be beneficial to try talking to her again. When we told Clara you were dead she shut down. She only talks to the guy who visits her and no one else. We are running out of options at this point," he admitted in a somber voice. "Will I be worried about you? Yes! Will I freak out from time to time? Yes! However, I know that in the end you will be safe and finally have your full freedom back."

"So you really think I should do it? You won't get mad at me for it?" I was in complete shock.

"I promise I won't get mad at you for this. It is still your decision, but I want you to know that I will stand behind you 100% no matter what you decide." He squeezed my hand.

"We still don't think this is a good idea. If Clara knows she's alive, she will tell Echo. What do you think Echo will do when she finds out?" Ben urged us to rethink.

"Why don't we play monopoly and I'll think about it tonight. I need a little bit of fun after trying to cut my finger off earlier. Dinner was wonderful tonight Ben. You aren't as good of a chef as I am, but I'll rank you a close second." I giggled as I got up from the table.

Logan got the game while we stacked the dinner dishes on the counter. The rest of the night was filled with laughter, Ben and Logan trying to cheat, and a lot of fun. By midnight we were all too tired to play, decided Kim was the winner, and went up to bed. I was nervous, but felt so safe snuggled into Logan's arms. It took awhile to fall asleep, but I managed.

The next morning I called and gave Chief Park's my answer. I told him I would do the interviews again, but I would need a week to prepare. He wasn't happy about my waiting so long but finally agreed. As much as I wanted out of the house and more answers, I wasn't ready to see Clara again. She had helped make my life a living hell.

Despite agreeing to start the interviews in a week, I was too nervous to go back to the police station. Luckily there were several issues and sightings of Echo near the police station, so they pushed the interview back an extra week.

A few nights before the interviews started back up, I paced the house and was up all night. I was startled by Logan when he came down to leave for work the next morning. He said he was meeting a few officers at the diner for breakfast, kissed me, and told me to go up and get a few hours of sleep. I dragged myself to my room. I was surprised to find a note on the bed. Logan was more romantic than I originally knew. I sat down and read it.

Hey Sexy,

I told Kim to take you out for breakfast. We thought you might want a break from cooking this morning, and deserve to get out of the house. I love you very much and have a nice dinner date planned. It will be just the two of us. Okay except for the whole bodyguard thing. There's a gift in the dresser, but please don't open it until it's time to get ready for dinner. I hope you have a wonderful day, and I will see you later.

Love,

Logan

I smiled and got ready for breakfast. "How did I get to be so lucky?" I thought to myself out loud, and walked down stairs. I was greeted by both Kim and Ben. Ben was obviously not going with as he was still in his pajamas. Kim grabbed my hand and we rushed out of the house like two school girls about to meet their first crushes. We giggled and joked the whole way to the Diner. I knew I had to be someone else while there, but I really wanted my favorite cheese fries. As I sat and stared at the menu, I pretended as if it's my first time there. I had to make this as real as possible if I wanted to survive my first diner outing as the new me.

"What can I get you two?" the tall lanky waitress asked while smacking her bubble gum annoyingly.

"I'll have coffee and the number one breakfast special please," Kim answered as her order was taken.

"I would like the chicken fried steak, mashed potatoes with lots of extra white gravy, and a coke. Thank you." I smiled and handed her the menu.

"Your order will be right up," she replied and walked away.

"So are you okay with the decision you made?"

"I think so. I'm nervous about it. I want a couple of the promises in writing. I don't care as much about myself, but I want to make sure Logan is safe," I whispered so no one else heard us.

"Understandable!" she whispered back. "Let's take our time and enjoy breakfast for now. We have plenty of time to talk shop later before your big date."

"Who will be standing by?" I asked curiously.

"Ben and I will be there. We will be at another table watching you though, so you'll have your privacy," she promised.

I begged for any information she had. "So where is he taking me tonight?"

She fidgeted with her napkin. "I promised him I wouldn't tell you. All I can say is that you will love it. This time you won't get a broken nose either."

We were both laughing when our food was brought to the table. The waitress stared at me for a moment before walking away and shaking her head. I was afraid for a moment that she recognized me, but I was glad to be wrong. We sat quietly and scarfed down our food. After we finished we sat for a while, talking and enjoying the freedom.

Elizabeth came over with a couple pieces of pie and sat down. "I heard your cousin was visiting Kim, so I had to bring her a piece of pie as a welcome."

"Thank you so much," I said with a huge smile.

Her pies were my favorite and I was glad she was playing along with my new identity, at least for the time being. We sat around chatting about the unusually warm weather and she filled me in on all of the latest gossip I had missed. By the time we got ready to leave it was close to lunch time. We ordered lunch for ourselves and the guys, and left for the station. When we got there Logan walked us into an empty interrogation room and we sat down for lunch.

"I'm glad we have some privacy to talk," I said.

Logan snuck a kiss. "I am too. How are you feeling honey?"

"Amazing! It's so wonderful to be out of the house." We exchanged another kiss. "I'm going to need some things in writing before I do this. I need to be sure we are safe before I rise from the dead." I laughed maniacally trying to be spooky.

"You're too funny. I'll go get the 'man in charge' so we can talk while we eat." Logan quickly left the room.

A moment later Logan and the leader of the FBI team entered the room and both took a seat. "I was told you have a question for me. What is it?"

"First of all I will need a few things in writing." I tried to be demanding.

"Like what?" he snapped back. "Why are you demanding things from us? We aren't the enemy."

"I never said you were the enemy. They should be easy enough demands. First of all I want you to promise that no matter what happens or how much Logan fights it, that he will be 100% protected. Second I no longer want an agent in the room when I'm with Clara."

"I can promise protection for both you and Logan. I cannot however promise to keep an agent out of the room. We need all of the information." He sounded pissed off at my demands.

"I will hand over my recordings at the end of each interview. Clara will not tell me everything if one of your agents is in the room. I've spent enough time with her to realize how she works," I justified.

"Fine, I will agree to these terms. I will also promise to make sure you have all copies of the interviews for yourself. Are you ready to start in a couple of days?" he asked me.

"I'm scared to death, but I'm ready. I'll be here in a couple of days to resume interviews," I explained.

"We would really like to be done with all this and the sooner you start, the sooner we can be done. Some of us have families to get home to," he rudely pointed out.

"I want my real identity back and to do a few things before I get started. Can I at least have another week?" I pretend to try and put things off longer just to test the waters.

"We will have everything ready by noon tomorrow. I'll see you in a couple of days. Are we done here?" he urged.

"I want it all in writing and then we are done here. Thank you for your time and for agreeing to my terms." I shook his hand and finished eating after he left the room.

We sat for another thirty minutes before he came in with my requests typed up and signed. I signed the papers and got up to leave. I kissed Logan and told him I would see him later. As we exited the room I yelled, "I'm back from the dead bitches! Get use to my face again!" Everyone ignored me and kept working.

Kim and I headed home to prepare for our wonderful date night with the men. At home I headed straight upstairs to get my shower, trying to avoid the box left for me on the dresser. I wasn't sure if it would be my style, or even a color I liked. I started getting nervous as this would be my first date in months. I finished my shower and headed down in my towel to get a cup of coffee. I wasn't getting a lot of sleep since coming home from the hospital, so I needed as much caffeine as possible.

Kim walked in having the same idea as me. "Great minds think alike. Have you opened the box yet?"

I shook my head and sipped my coffee. "Not yet. I don't know why but I'm nervous about opening it. I feel like a lunatic tonight. Why do I feel like this is a blind date?"

Kim laughed a little. "It's your first real time out of the house since you were revealed to the world as dead. It is very normal to be nervous. Just go drink your coffee, get your hair done, and put on the beautiful dress I helped pick out."

"You helped him pick it out? I feel a little better now." I smiled as she gave me the "get your ass in gear" look. "Okay, okay I am going right now."

I dried my hair, and put on some much needed makeup. The dark circles under my eyes were hard to conceal, but I managed to do it. I followed up with a soft lilac eye shadow, a small amount of blush, and decided to wait on the lipstick. No need to ruin a dress before I even get to wear it out. I sighed as I looked in the mirror at my new short pixie cut and frowned when I realized I had no idea how to style it. I opted out of anything other than making sure I didn't have any hairs sticking up. Next was getting dressed. I slowly open the box to reveal a floor length thick satin dress. It was beautiful shade of light pastel purple. It was form fitting, with three quarter length sleeves, and a v-neck that came down slightly between the breasts. The v-neck was lined with flowers in a darker shade of purple. I carefully put on the dress, but before I could go look at myself in the mirror, Kim entered the room with two smaller boxes. I opened the first to reveal a pair of purple 'fuck me' pumps that perfectly matched the flowers. The second box was filled with a small clutch purse made of the same fabric, and a note from Logan.

Hey there Sexy,

I hope everything is to your liking. I had a little bit of help from Kim picking it all out. I have a very special surprise for you tonight and I can't wait to see how beautiful you look. Your ride will be there at 6 pm so make sure you're ready. I hope I make all your dreams come true tonight.

Forever Yours,

Logan

It took everything I had inside me to keep from crying. I focused on finishing getting myself ready. Then I changed out my purse, put on my shoes, and headed into the bathroom to finally take a look at myself in the mirror. I decided to skip the lipstick and go downstairs where Kim was waiting by the door. I gave her a hug, and realized it was time to go.

When I walked outside, I saw a white stretch limo waiting for us. Standing next to the limo I could see Ben and Logan, both of them grinning from ear to ear. It was just like prom night. Kim and I looked at each other and smiled before joining the two men.

Logan pulled me in close and kissed me before whispering in my ear. "You look absolutely amazing. I hope you like my next surprise."

"Thank you sweetie, I know I'll love whatever you have planned. As long as I am with you, the night will be perfect." I took his hand and he helped me into the limo.

The limo was filled with small talk and happiness and I was full of more love than I thought was possible. I held Logan's hand and put my head on his shoulder. It would be the first time we went out since I was shot and since he proposed to me. I felt as if we were surrounded by magic. When the limo stopped I was confused about where we were. We had pulled up in front the police department.

"I thought we were going out for a romantic evening. The police station is not my idea of romance," I thought to myself out loud.

The three of them laughed and Logan took my hand, helped me out of the limo, and walked me into the station.

"This is just a short pit stop. We have reservations for dinner but we needed to stop by and pick up a few things first. It will just take a few minutes I promise."

As we walked inside, I was taken aback by the new look. They decorated the room in white and purple Christmas lights, vases full of flowers, and everyone was in their dress blues.

I stopped walking and stared in amazement. "What's going on here?"

"Well." Logan paused for a moment. "I was hoping you would agree to marry me tonight. Kim said you didn't want to wait too long. If it's too soon we can wait. If you still want a huge wedding when all of this craziness is over we can do that too. I know it's not the most romantic place in the world to get married, but all of your friends are here. Okay not all of them, but all of your friends from town are."

"I do want a big wedding, but this is perfect. I couldn't think of a better group of people to be surrounded by when I finally marry the man of my dreams." I had to fight back the tears.

Everyone gathered around for a short ceremony. We both sounded like blubbering idiots as we said our impromptu vows. No one in the station was able to hold back their tears as we were pronounced husband and wife. It may not have been a big wedding with a thousand guests, neither of our parents could be there, and my closest friends were five hours away, but I wouldn't have traded it for anything in the world.

After the ceremony we hung around for a while chatting with the guests and eating our wedding pie. Yes, we had pie instead of cake. Elizabeth made pies for the occasion but promised me the biggest wedding cake ever when we had a bigger ceremony. I gathered both of the single women together. But before tossing my bouquet I separated it into two, and then tossed them behind me. We gave goodbye hugs, and headed back to the limo so we wouldn't miss our dinner reservations.

We spent the evening at a beautiful new restaurant, eating, dancing, and talking about the future. We had to leave early when I started to get sick to my stomach. Logan stayed up with me all night taking care of me and making sure I had everything I needed.

"This is not how I imagined spending my wedding night," I forced out in between puking.

"Not what I had in mind either but I will do anything and everything to make you feel better." He kissed my forehead and rubbed my back.

When I was still sick and unable to keep anything down the next morning, Logan called and made me a doctor's appointment. At the doctors they did all of the normal tests before sending me over to the hospital so I could get some fluids. An hour or so after I arrived, my doctor came in to tell me the results of my many tests.

"Well I think I know what's causing all of this." He paused and smiled. "Congratulations! You have a little one on the way. I'll have an ultrasound done to make sure everything is going the way it should. For now you just need a lot of rest."

Logan's bottom jaw dropped and he couldn't say a word. I thought the doctor was messing with me and managed to get the words, "you're joking right?" out of my mouth.

"I'm not joking. According to your hCG count I'd say you're about a month or so along give or take a few days," he explained.

"Is it normal to be this sick?" I asked.

He smiled trying to reassure me. "From what I hear you had a great time last night. Morning sickness can be hell on a woman and alcohol intensifies it. Don't freak out about drinking. You're not the first woman to drink and not know they were pregnant. I'm sure you have nothing to worry about. I'll arrange for your ultrasound and get some more fluids in you before sending you home to rest in your own bed."

Kim and Ben came in to visit for awhile. "So has the doctor figured out what's wrong yet? Do you have the flu or something? What's wrong with Logan?"

"You'll have to excuse him. I think he's still in a state of shock." I smiled and squeezed Logan's hand. "We do know what's wrong. I'm pregnant."

Kim leaned down and hugged me while her eyes filled with tears. "That's amazing news. Guess we need to step up security for you. We can't let anything happen to the little one."

Ben walked over to Logan and tried to get his attention. "Dude, are you going to be okay? Snap out of it man. You're going to be a father soon. Man up!"

Logan finally let the news sink in, and seemed to be surprised at the fact that we had company. "I'm sorry guys. I didn't know you came in. I'm going to be a father."

After spending a few more hours in the emergency room I finally had permission to leave. I spent the next week in bed with Logan waiting on me hand and foot. It was nice to be pampered, but at the same time I was so annoyed I just wanted to smack him. I tried my best to be nice to him, and when I did yell he just shrugged it off. Being stuck in bed and having him take such good care of me, made me fall deeper in love with him.

I managed to make it a week before I demanded he let me do something on my own. "I'm pregnant, not dying sweetie. I lot of pregnant women do things for themselves."

"I just don't want you stressed out at all." He held my hands almost begging me to let him keep me in bed.

"Being stuck in that bed is stressing me out. Besides, I have serial killer to continue interviewing. If you want this baby to be safe, you'll let me get back to work. I was supposed to start last week. I will call and set things up for tomorrow. I can't live my life in fear anymore. I will get all the information needed to catch that crazy bitch, and put her behind bars where she belongs," I said trying to convince him.

"Fine, but I get to spoil my new wife for one more day."

He laid down next to me on the bed, put his hands on my belly, and started talking to it. "Hi little one. It's your daddy. I can't wait to meet you and hold you in my arms. I love you so much and I'm going to spoil you rotten."

I called the station later that day to let them know I was feeling better and would be in the next day to start the interviews again. Chief Parks tried to talk me out of it knowing that I was pregnant but I assured him that everything was fine and I could handle it. He gave in after 20 minutes and told me to be there by 10:00am.

I hung up the phone and screamed. "Why is everyone treating me like I'm a fucking invalid? I'm not going to break."

"There are those raging hormones we were waiting for." Kim laughed as she headed to the kitchen.

I got up and stomped down the stairs like a two year old. "It's not my damn hormones!" I yelled. "It happens to be the fact that everyone thinks that just because I'm pregnant I can longer think or do things for myself. I can do my own laundry, take a shower by myself, cook my own meals, and I sure as fuck can go back to work on my own."

"I take it Logan is still hovering a little too much?" Ben asked as he walked joined us in the kitchen.

"Don't get me wrong. I love that he wants me to be comfortable. It's sweet how helpful he has been but I can't be wrapped in bubble wrap 24/7." I sounded like I was whining.

Logan spent the rest of the day moping around and avoiding me. I was upset that I had hurt his feelings but I was happy to be doing things on my own again. At dinner he was still avoiding me so I sat down on the couch hoping to make him talk to me.

"I'm sorry I was so mean. I lost my temper and I shouldn't have," I tried to apologize to him the best I could.

"I know. I shouldn't hover so much and I deserved it. I was just trying to give you some space," he finally conceded.

I grabbed his face and looked him in the eyes. "I never want you to think that I need this much space. I always want you around. No matter what I say, or how much I throw a fit. I never want you to feel unwanted or unloved. I also want you to promise me that we will never go to bed angry." I pulled his face towards mine and kissed him.

"I thought you wanted me to leave you alone for a while. I thought I was being nice. Don't worry, I promise to always work things out and talk to you no matter what." He kissed me again.

Chapter Fifteen

I over slept the next morning and Kim had to wake me up. I rushed around to get ready, grabbing a bottle of Sprite and some saltines to eat on the way. Halfway there I realized I forgot my recorder and we had to turn around and go back. I noticed someone running through the back yard as we pulled into the long driveway.

"Forget the recorder Kim. We need to get out of here fast!" I shouted while pointing towards whoever it was running away from the house.

Kim backed out of the driveway quickly while calling her boss. "We need someone at Brooke's house fast. We were on our way back to pick up her recorder when she noticed someone running away from the back of the house."

She nodded a bit as she continued to speed away. "I understand sir."

"Yes…. We are on our way there right now. See you there." She hung up.

"I'm sorry that I couldn't see who it was. I'm glad we went back though or something could have happened."

"It's going to be okay. The FBI and some state troopers are on their way to check out the house now. We will place more guards outside from now on. I'll get you into the station and while you give your statement to my boss, I will go and buy you a new recorder. Try and relax a little. I won't let anything happen to you."

When we got to the police station I was greeted by Logan who had been pacing outside the front door. He ran up and wrapped his arms around me as soon as he saw me. "Thank God you're alright. I was so worried. All I knew was that they sent all man power they could over to the house. No one would tell me anything."

"We need to get her statement real quick Logan. Then you can smother her in kisses," Detective James said as he lightly took my arm and lead me inside.

I told Detective James and an FBI agent everything that happened that morning.

"Kim had to wake me up this morning, as I overslept. I was in such a hurry, and felt so rushed, that I forgot my recorder. I didn't notice it until after we left. Realizing I forgot it, I asked Kim to take me back to get it. As we turned into the driveway, I saw someone running away from the house. I couldn't tell who it was. I'm so sorry. I don't even know if the person I saw was male or female."

"It's ok. We will stop at nothing to find whoever it was. I know it will be hard, but please try and stay calm. We don't want you to be too upset."

I knew I couldn't go back to my own home until Echo was behind bars. I started to fear that I would never again feel safe. For the first time since all of this started I was more than terrified.

I ran out of the room and into Logan's arms. Even then I didn't feel safe. I was more determined than ever to get to the bottom of all this madness. I knew I had to fight no matter what the cost would be. She must pay for what she did to my family, my husband, and to me. My fear turned to hatred, and then into dedication. I paced the floor as I waited for Kim to return with my recorder. They went ahead and brought Clara up to an interrogation room and as she walked passed me our eyes met. For a moment my body filled with rage as I stared at the one person who could finally give me the answers I needed. My gaze was broken as Kim came into view.

She handed me two recorders. "I wasn't sure which one to get so I got both of them. Are you sure you want to do this? It's not too late to change your mind."

"Thank you, these will work perfectly," I said with a smile. "I'm not backing down. I will get the information needed even if I have to strangle it out of the bitch. She will not win. I refuse to let them win."

Kim pulled me to the side. "If you keep talking about killing her they won't let you do this. I understand how hurt, angry, and scared you are, but you have to keep your cool. Take a few deep breaths before going in there."

"I know I need to calm down." I did as she recommended and took several deep breaths. "I can do this. I won't let her get to me."

I took another deep breath and walk into the room. I placed the recorder on the table, pressed play, and looked up to see Clara smiling at me.

"I thought you were dead?" she said matter of factly. "I had a feeling they were lying to me. I love the new look though. That hairstyle fits you perfectly."

"Cut the bullshit Clara. I know you and Echo have a messenger delivering notes back and forth. They are searching your cell now. What I want to know is, who he is to the two of you. I also want to know where Echo is hiding," I demanded in a strong, firm tone.

"All in good time Brooke. You promised to listen to my entire story. I'm going to hold you to that. The sooner we finish this, the sooner I tell you what I know about her."

"I really don't have time for any of this. I need answers now, not later. You give me the correct information to find and arrest Echo and I will listen to the rest of your stories. Do you understand me?" I fought the urge to once again strangle her.

"We do things my way or I walk. You are not in charge, no matter how much you think or wish you were." She leaned back in her chair.

"I will listen, but you better make it quick." I reluctantly gave in knowing it may be my only option.

"I'm glad you see things my way. Now where were we?" She sat thinking for a few minutes, knowing how angry she was making me. "I remember now. Victim number five. That was Linda Garret. She was just 21 years old, with beautiful long red hair, and boring hazel eyes. I took her on July 29th, but I won't bore you with the how I made it possible. Linda looked like she was from the sixties, with her straight, long red hair, tie dyed tank top, bell bottom jeans, and flip flops. I learned she was visiting from Edgewater, Colorado and was staying with her cousin."

"What was your reason for taking her?" I tried to act interested.

"That's a very good question. It's a simple answer. I don't like hippies. They are dirty disgusting people who never bathe and never shave. Always 'trippin' on some kind of drug and they care more about plants and trees than other humans. I did the world a favor by getting rid of another nasty human."

"Is that really how you see it?"

"Yes, that is really how I see it," she explained mockingly.

"You don't have to be a bitch about it. I'm just asking questions," I snapped, once again losing my cool.

Kim shot me a look and shook her head. I knew what she meant without any words being spoken. I had to stay calm.

"On day one I kept it simple. I used a branding iron and told her since she liked animals so much, I would brand her like cattle. I used it on her twelve to fifteen times. I can't remember now, but I do remember the wonderful smell of her flesh burning each time I placed it against her skin. It was a beautiful smell to me." Once again she smiled as she remembered the smell.

Picturing the flesh being burned and imagining the smell of it burning made my stomach churn. I fought the urge to vomit. I didn't want her to think she was getting to me.

"Feeling a little queasy today? Do you want to take a break already?"

I took a deep breath and looked her in the eyes. "I'm fine. I just forgot breakfast this morning and I think I've got the flu kicking in. Keep going."

She flashed a smile my way and continued. "I took my time with branding her. I did it once every half hour. It was more fun to let it drag on longer. Just as she would start to relax a bit, I would heat up the iron and press it firmly against her skin. God, I love remembering this victim. It was so magical to me. A real masterpiece if I do say so myself. Do you have the pictures of her dead body? I'd love to see it again."

"We do have photos, but you're not allowed to look at them. Sorry to disappoint you," I scoffed knowing it would piss her off even more.

"Just as well, the images are still pretty fresh in my mind," she gloated.

"On day two I researched where to stab someone and not kill them. I wanted to avoid hitting a major organ or any major veins. It was very easy to find all the information online. Did you know you can even learn how to make explosives out of materials found in your home online?"

I rolled my eyes and sighed. "Yes I know that. You can learn to do anything online if you know how to search properly."

She let out a loud chuckle. "I thought about blowing her up, but realized that would be way too messy. I didn't want to spend that long cleaning her off of my walls, floors, and ceilings." She paused for a moment as if the thought made her sick.

"I grabbed my trusty paring knife after deciding it was less likely to hit an artery or any organs. I stabbed her first in the left side, and quickly stitched it up. Her screaming was like music to my ears. The more she screamed, the happier I was," Clara admitted with a grin.

"After stitching up the first spot, I stabbed her right foot. Again I stitched up the wound. I repeated this 8 more times. Each time I stitched slower and slower making the pain last longer. I spent about five hours torturing her. After the final stitch she spit on me. I was so pissed off that I punched her repeatedly until she passed out."

"I notice you didn't really mention going to work. Did you have a job, or was there family money?" I scrutinized.

"To answer your question in full, I had money from selling all of my mother's belongings, and her house. I also had a large amount of money that my grandma left me. I didn't need to work because there was enough money to live off of for the rest of my life."

"That explains a lot. I was wondering how you bought food and paid your bills. Now I know," I uttered sarcastically.

"On day three I started by sharpening a large knife in front of her. I could tell by the look in her eyes that she was thinking I was going to stab her again."

"Was that your plan or did you plan on skinning her like you did your victim Randy Dugan?" I quizzed.

"I did not stab or skin her. Well not exactly. I finished sharpening the knife and looked at her with a wicked grin. I grabbed a big chunk of her hair and started scalping her. I continued until not one strand of hair was left on her head. I knew she had spent most of her life growing out her hair, and wanted to take that away. She didn't deserve that hair."

"I left her alone long enough to fix a sandwich. I ate in front of her knowing how hungry she was. I waved the last bite right in front of her face, and as she tried to bite for it, she bit me instead. That's when I knew I needed to teach her a lesson. I searched through the 'toy' drawer and grabbed a pair of pliers. One by one as I forced her mouth open, I pulled tooth after tooth, until all she had left were her molars and wisdom teeth. She spat on me again, this time with a mouth full of blood. As you know, that's not a good thing to do. I boxed both of her ears repeatedly until I could see blood running out of them and down her neck. It was such a wonderful thing to do. I wish I had thought of doing it sooner."

"What was the reason for boxing her ears? Did you think it would calm her down?"

"No, I did it because it was something painful to do." She rolled her eyes at me once again.

"That night I went out with Echo and partied. I left Linda down in the basement for two more days before going back to torture her more. That day I took several empty glass bottles and broke them over her head. I swept the glass into a smaller area and devised a plan to make her walk on it. I knew it could go badly, but I wanted to try something new. So, while she was knocked out I removed the straps holding her to the table, and tightly tied her hands behind her back. When she finally awoke I started making her walk on the broken glass towards the door. I held a machete to her throat. What I didn't realize is that I didn't make the knots tight enough and she managed to get her hands free. She turned so quickly that I didn't notice she was free until after she punched me in the face."

"You mean to tell me that you actually made a mistake? One of your victims almost got away? That's not like you. How did you stop her?" I relished in the thought of her finally making a mistake.

"If you're going to keep interrupting me I won't continue. Are you going to shut up and listen or am I leaving?" she barked at me.

"Go ahead Clara. I'll be quiet for now." I chuckled in amusement.

She continued with the story. "I quickly got to my feet and ran out of the room. I grabbed a hold of a pitchfork leaning against the wall, and as I ran up the stairs after her I stabbed it into her back. She dropped and slid down the stairs causing the pitchfork to come loose and fall out. We struggled for what seemed like an hour. Exchanging punches before I dragged her back into the room, closed the door behind us, and slit her throat with the machete. The walls and floor were covered in blood splatter and a pool of blood as she bled out on the floor. I left her there and retrieved the wheelbarrow so I could dump her body with the others. I spent the next week cleaning up blood, hair, teeth, glass, and bits of her scalp in the room, and getting it ready for my next victim."

"Let's take a break to eat and then you can tell me about the last victim," I suggested knowing I needed a break for a little bit.

"Sounds like a great idea to me," she agreed.

I slowly got up and walked out of the room. As soon as the door closed behind me I bolted for the bathroom and threw up. Kim came in and handed me a wet paper towel. I knew Logan had sent her in to check on me.

"I'm fine. I'm just not handling all the gruesome details as well this time. I only have to sit through one more victim and then hopefully, if all goes well, she will tell me what we need to know," I tried to convince both of us.

"I didn't say anything. Logan is the one worried about whether or not you can handle all of this right now. I know you can do it. You're the strongest woman I have ever met. Most people would have given up when they lost a parent." Kim put her arm around me as we left the bathroom and headed out to give the men our food orders.

I hugged Logan and smiled sweetly so he knew nothing was wrong. "Can I have a mushroom swiss burger with ranch dressing and cheese fries with extra cheese and ranch please?"

"On a ranch dressing kick I see." He laughed at my odd taste. "You can have anything you want."

"I'm not sure what's so funny. I've always loved ranch dressing. It's not really that odd. I know a lot of people who eat ranch on everything. It's not like I'm asking for pickles and ice cream. That would be odd and gross. Oh… I want hot sauce too," I shouted as he walked out of the building.

It only took about 20 minutes for them to get back with our food since they called in the order on the way. We sat in the interrogation room and ate. No one talked for most of the time and instead they stared at me while I shoveled the food in my mouth. I stopped when I felt all eyes on me.

"What's wrong? Do I have food on my face?" I grabbed a napkin and covered my mouth.

"Nope, no food on your face. We've just never seen you eat so fast before. We were just making sure you weren't going to start eating us next," Ben tried to joke.

"That's not funny Ben," I snapped. "I missed breakfast, and the baby is hungry. I plan on getting nice and fat this pregnancy." I looked over at Logan and smiled.

"You keep eating like that and you just might gain 300 lbs," Kim snorted.

Logan looked at me lovingly. "You eat all you want. Even if you weigh 800 lbs I'll still love you. As long as you're happy, I'm happy."

"Thank you baby." I stuck my tongue out at Ben and Kim.

"They're just jealous of your ability to eat after listening to a crazy psycho bitch. Neither of them can handle it. They have weak stomachs and are wusses." He leaned over and kissed my cheek.

"I know they are. I'm one tough cookie. OMG! Now I want cookies," I cried.

We all started laughing so hard none of us could finish eating. I prepared myself for the next part of the interview as I helped clean up our lunch mess. Logan brought in a few Sprites and kissed me as he went back to work. While I finished my interview for the day, he planned to make arrangements for a safer place to stay. He knew me well enough to know I would be too afraid to sleep at home until Echo had been caught. I quietly waited as an officer went back down to get Clara.

Clara was cuffed once again to the floor and table. She didn't give me time to do anything except hit record on my recorder before she started her next story.

"I know you're anxious to get started so I'll just jump right in. Victim number six was my oldest and the most annoying. He was 72 year old Lenny Romin. He was about 5' 10" with messy white hair. If I remember correctly he was from Salem, Arkansas and I'm pretty sure he was one of those people who give Arkansas a bad name. I always heard people joke about not dating their family because they weren't from Arkansas, but to be honest I think he was a product of incest. I lured him to my house on August 19th. On the first night I tried to strike up a conversation with him. He was so fucking boring that all I remember is that he was just passing through town. He blabbed on and on for hours about how he hated everyone that wasn't white. He wanted all of them to suffer and die slow deaths. After about 3 hours I gave up and left him alone in the room. He made me want to bash my head into the wall."

"At least I know you're not racist. See, you do have one good quality."

"I do hate racists who think they are better than anyone else. I forgot to mention my first round of torture for him. He was left alone in the room with rap music blaring on the speakers. What better way to torture a racist than to force him to listen to the music created by those he hates most?" She couldn't stop laughing, and to be honest I joined her.

"That's a new and interesting way to torture someone. I like that idea."

"So the next day I joined him in the room, and even tried

my hand at rapping. The look on his face was beyond annoyed. I decided to start the day by beating him gang style. It just seemed to be very fitting for the situation. I spent several hours beating the living shit out of him. As I hit him with brass knuckles, a baseball bat, and a tire iron, I was delighted to watch his bones break, and see all of the blood splatter all over the room. I was covered in blood droplets and small pieces of flesh by the time I finished, and he never screamed or yelled. Instead he kept droning on and on about his hatred for so many races. Do you know how angry it makes me to hear someone talking about whites being the one true race?"

"I would have beaten the shit out of him myself. No room for that kind of hatred in this world. There are enough psychopaths already."

"That was a low blow Brooke." I could see the anger in her eyes from my statement.

"Let's get back to this victim. I left the music on for the second night. As I tried to fall asleep I made up my mind that I couldn't take it anymore. I had to think of a good way to finish him off once and for all. It was then that I remembered the three dogs I had recently rescued. Two of them were pit bulls and one was a Rottweiler. I saved them from a vet's office before they could be put down. The dogs were bred for fighting and I convinced the vet that I could rehabilitate them. I kept them in the barn in separate cages and was working on calming them down."

"So you care about dogs and want to save them? Most serial killers start by killing animals before graduating to people. It was nice of you to try and help keep the dogs alive."

"Blah, blah, blah! I'm nice and I have a heart somewhere in there. I've heard it all before. Don't get all sappy on me. You haven't heard what I did yet."

"Apparently it wasn't a good thing."

"It was a horribly wonderful thing." She let out a deep breath and grinned. "I waited until the next night before drugging him. I had a friend steal enough drugs to kill all three dogs."

"How did you convince her to steal them for you?"

"I told her the dogs were restless and trying to chew their own legs off. So she agreed to help me. I used some of the drugs on Lenny to knock him out. While the meds were starting to kick in I ran to the store and bought supplies to make several pizzas. I called and invited Echo over when I got home. I knew I needed help getting Lenny up to the barn. While we made a pizza for dinner, I explained to her that I needed help and reminded her that she owed me. She was angry that I didn't ask her to help sooner, but agreed to help anyway. After dinner, we dragged him outside and closed up the barn. The two of us spent a half hour gluing pepperonis to Lenny's body."

"You glued food to his body? That sounds a little crazy."

"The whole time we were doing it the dogs were in their cages going nuts. They could smell the meat and wanted it more than anything because I hadn't fed them in 2 days. I ran back inside and grabbed my gun just in case the dogs got a little too wild. We sat talking while we waited for Lenny to start coming too and placed a gag in his mouth before we stood on top of the large cages and released the dogs. The dogs ran right for him. It was such a beautiful sight to see the pain and fear in his eyes as the dogs ripped through his flesh and tore him from limb to limb. There were body parts, blood, and his organs all over the place. It only took the dogs 45 minutes to eat almost all of him. After that they started turning on each other. I knew the dogs could not be stopped at this point, so I sadly shot them each in the head. We placed Lenny's leftover body parts, what few there were, in the hole with the others. After that we dug three large holes and buried the dogs."

"At least you gave the dogs a proper burial."

"It was the least I could do for all of the help and joy they gave me."

"I'm sorry but I think that's all for today. I'll make arrangements for tomorrow. When I come in I expect you to tell me everything you currently know about Echo and where she's hiding."

"Sounds like a date."

I turned off the recorder and left the room. I was met by the lead FBI agent and as promised, I handed him the recorder. I let him know that it was just about Clara's last two victims.

"You can keep this recording. Right now all we want is information on Echo." He handed the recorder back.

"I will come in tomorrow to get that information for you. Right now I just need a safe place to get some sleep."

"We're still discussing that issue Brooke. We won't let anything happen to you, and that's a promise. I'm just sorry we didn't have more agents and officers guarding your house this morning."

"I just have to come to terms with the fact that I won't be safe again until Echo is dead or behind bars."

I took a seat at Logan's empty desk and waited for him to finish his meeting. All I could do was pray that a new place could be found for us. My mind raced with what ifs, and why didn't I's. Maybe my father would still be alive if I had made different choices. Why didn't I just refuse to do the interviews? What if I had postponed my visit? Would Echo still have killed my father? Would I still have ended up shot? No matter what I did, the questions kept coming. It was too late anyway. Nothing I said or did could change that. My life was already spiraling so far out of control. For the sake of my baby I had to focus on the future, and work as hard as possible to make my life better. Besides, if Clara cooperated it would all be over soon.

I was startled by the sudden hands on my shoulders. "How are you feeling sweetie?"

"I'm doing well, just a little tired. Do we have a safe place to go yet?"

"They are still working on that. Tonight we will go home."

"NO!" I yelled. "I can't go back there. Not until I know Echo can't hurt us. She's already made it past the police before."

"We will be safe. They promised to have guards stationed at every door, several walking the yard, and outside of the bedroom doors. Hopefully a new temporary place will be found tomorrow."

"I'll just sleep here at your desk. It will be better than being at home too afraid to close my eyes. I'm telling you I just can't go back there."

"Don't be like that Brooke. You can handle it for one night. We can get up early and come back here for the interview. After that it's only a matter of time before they catch her. Try to stay calm please."

"Fine, but only for one night, and if anything happens I promise that you will pay for it the rest of your life."

"I get it. Keep you safe or fear your wrath."

"I'm glad we're on the same page. Now take me to get food and sleep."

"It will be a few minutes. Agents are sweeping the house to make sure it's still safe for us. I already called in our order for fried chicken and french fries at Pizza Express. I know it's your favorite chicken, and you keep telling me it's the best chicken in the world. We can pick it up on the way home. Just sit and relax for a little longer."

"You're such a meanie poo poo head," I joked, pretending to give him a dirty look.

Everyone in the room looked at me sitting in the chair with my arms folded, sticking my tongue out at Logan. I knew I looked like a child, but it was better than yelling at everyone and barking orders, although, that's what I really wanted to do. I was so angry all I wanted to do was hit something. I pictured Echo crossing a street in front of me and me speeding up to run her over. The thought of it made me smile. I knew I would never have the guts to really do it, but the thought was good enough at the time.

Chapter Sixteen

It took several more hours before we were able to return home. The restaurant was closed and we had to settle for sandwiches. I only ate half of mine and went up to bed so I could try and get some sleep. I was awake until 2:00am and was tired the next morning when Logan woke me up. He brought me breakfast in bed. It wasn't much, but I was so happy I didn't have to cook.

"You were right Honey. You do make the best toast ever," I said jokingly.

"I'm a genius when it comes to toast."

"You sure are." I smiled and took another bite. "I hope we get to sleep somewhere else tonight. I was up late because I was so worried."

"I really don't know. Maybe Clara will give you enough information and they will catch Echo tonight. We may be free to go back to a normal life soon."

"She better or I just might snap. I'm under way too much stress right now and it's not good on the baby."

"You need to finish eating and get dressed so we can go and get some information."

"What's with the we? I'm the one who has to get Clara to spill the beans."

"I want to be in there today. I don't have to work and I

don't want to stay here. Since I can't go shopping or anything else normal, I thought maybe you would let me sit in on the interview today."

"This may sound stupid, but I have to ask Clara if it's okay with her. I have to follow her rules or I'll never get her to talk. If you do join us you have to remember no talking. She hates when others jump in on her conversations."

"I promise I won't say a word to anyone."

"Thank you Sweetie! I want to talk to the lead agent before the interview today. I'm going to go get ready and I'll meet you downstairs."

I took a quick shower, dried my hair, threw on some old comfy clothes, and joined what looked like a small army in the living room. They were talking when I started down the stairs and quit when I entered the room. It was almost as if they were talking about me. I shrugged it off and headed to the kitchen to make some tea. I didn't need any more stress.

"Are you about ready to go?" Kim asked with a smile.

"Almost, I think. I just want to make some tea since I can't have any coffee." I returned her smile.

"Just let me know when you are ready. Logan and a couple agents are going to leave now. We agreed it was safer if the two of you didn't travel together for the time being."

"Alright I guess I will go along with whatever you guys decide. Why did everyone stop talking when I entered the room? It makes me feel uncomfortable."

"No Brooke. I promise they were not talking about you. They were talking about a lead they may have on Echo and didn't want to further upset you."

"So they were just trying to be nice? You promise?"

"That's all it was. Let's get going so you can have your meeting before the interview."

The ride to the station was more uncomfortable than ever before. I didn't feel like talking with people I didn't even know. Kim and one of the agents were in the front, and I had an agent on either side of me in the backseat. I felt like a prisoner in transport from one prison to another. Ironically enough, I was on my way to the police station. Even surrounded by FBI agents I still felt unsafe. Nothing would make me feel better except the arrest of Echo Shay.

I was immediately taken into the interrogation room where Logan, Chief Parks, and the lead FBI agent were waiting. All of the men looked confused as to why I wanted a meeting and I knew they probably wouldn't listen to what I had to say.

"I know you're all confused, and I want to thank you for meeting with me."

"What's this about Brooke?" the chief asked in a slightly annoyed tone.

"As you know, I have spent many days shut in this room interviewing and listening to Clara. From what I have gathered so far, all of the murders were very gruesome. She laughed and smiled at times, but for some reason my gut is telling me she didn't do any of the killing alone. While I do know that she helped kill my mother, and might have helped with dumping bodies, I do not think she actually did all of this. The bodies were dumped in a random hole on her property. There was no sign of remorse in any way, shape, or form. Am I correct so far?"

"You are correct about showing no sign of remorse in the dumping of the bodies, but how did you conclude that Clara didn't kill the victims or had help?" The agent questioned me with a confused look.

"I noticed a few things during several of the interviews."

"What kind of things?" Logan asked.

"On several occasions I noticed that she was fighting back tears. That's not the sign of a guilty person. I think she may have been there, but I don't think she did it. I also noticed that she would cringe whenever she said the name Echo. It was as if the name itself brought pain and fear to her. I could be wrong, but I think in a way, Clara was also a victim. She may be taking credit because her fear of Echo is far too great."

"That's possible, but for now we just want answers about the location of Echo. Any information you can get for us would be greatly appreciated," the agent explained half heartedly.

"I'll do what I can. I just need a few minutes to get everything ready before you bring her up. I brought my video camera as a secondary way of recording the interviews. That way maybe you can see what I'm talking about."

"I'll go get us something to drink and talk to the guys while you get ready," Logan suggested and kissed me on the top of my head before exiting the room with the others.

I knew they wouldn't understand, so I set out to prove my theory. I set up the camera facing the front of her chair, and pulled out my recorder. After I was sure everything was ready, I let Logan know so they could bring Clara in.

"What's with the camera?" she asked as they cuffed her to the table.

"I just thought it would be a nice change. You know in case they turn your story into a movie and all. I would also like to know if you have any objections to Officer Galloway sitting in on the interview. I told him it was up to you."

"I guess it's ok, but he's not allowed to talk. This is an interview between the two of us and not him."

"Thank you for allowing him to be here." I motioned for the guard to get Logan.

Logan walked in and hit record on the camera for me. "I will only say this. Thank you Clara for allowing me to be in here. I will not say anything else for the rest of the interview."

"You're welcome. Now what questions do you have for me Brooke?"

I took a deep breath before asking my first question. "What can you tell us about Echo that may help us understand the way she thinks?"

"I can only tell you what I've learned over the years. I know she had a rough life. Her parents divorced when she was 4, but continued to live in the same house until she was 15. It was not the ideal living arrangement. She also had an identical twin sister named Eva. She hated Eva with all of her being. While Echo was always in trouble for this or that, to their parents Eva could do no wrong. She was nice, polite, minded her P's and Q's, and it made Echo very angry and very jealous. It's also the reason she was always hanging out with me. Her mom once called my grandma and begged her to keep Echo for the entire summer. She said the sisters were fighting so much that she just needed a break. What a great mom, huh?"

"That's so sad. How could any parent send their kid away like that? No wonder she has issues."

"Right? Anyway, by the time Echo was a freshman I was a senior. We both got teased and picked on because of our friendship. Teachers always asked her why she couldn't be more like her sister, and her parents asked the same thing. It got to her you know. A person can only take so much before they snap. Needless to say we both dropped out of school. Then there was the whole incident with your mother." Clara started to cry a little. "Let's not get into that again. I will regret it till the day I die. Which, let's face it, could be soon. After I turned 18, I got a job and my own apartment. Echo's parents agreed to let her stay with me since they could no longer handle her. The only good thing they did was help with the bills and food. I may not agree with everything Echo has ever done, but I can understand why she turned out that way. When your own parents turn on you instead of seriously trying to help and pawn you off on other people, you're bound to end up screwed up beyond repair." She pauses for a moment trying to calm herself and fight back more tears. "She started working at age 16 and because I wanted Echo to have a better life, she got her GED at 17. She then started working for some older man who was a computer programmer. He had no children so he passed his knowledge on to her. He taught her everything he knew."

"She could have been somebody important if she had made better decisions. Echo is not some stupid high school dropout. In fact she had an IQ of 159. About 2 years ago her parents were selling their house. The man she worked for had died several months earlier and left her a lot of money, his house, and all of his belongings, so she bought her parents' house and also kept his. She spent most of her time at the house she grew up in and worked out of the other house. I moved into my grandma's house after she died, and invited my mother to stay with me. Then my mom had the 'accident' and I took over the house and money."

"Does Echo's other house have any secret rooms? According to police documents it looks a lot larger on the outside than it does inside."

"That's one thing I don't know. I've only seen the outside of it once when I picked her up for dinner. I'm sorry I can't help more with that."

"It's okay. Does she have a boyfriend or anyone she sees on a regular basis?"

"She said she was seeing someone, but wouldn't tell me his name. I know he's only 17 and according to her, adores everything she does. He's not from Brines though. He's a 6' tall God, with the perfect body, and he's amazing in bed. At least that's what she told me. Wait! I remember she said he has chestnut brown hair, and two different colored eyes. Not like a blue and a green though. Like one dark brown and one very light brown. I've never met him, so I don't know if it's true or not."

"Is there anywhere else she could pull off murdering people?"

"I know her dad used to own a gas station off the highway as you're leaving town, but I don't know if he sold it before he went out of business. I do know that she has cameras everywhere. She even told me about how on numerous occasions she hacked into the city cameras downtown. I still don't know how she did it without getting caught, but she did. She placed cameras around both of her houses, and can track whenever anyone enters. I would be extra careful anywhere they check for her."

"Do they only need to be careful because of the cameras or is she capable of more than just spying?"

"I believe she is capable of much more than spying. She learned how to make bombs and other explosives over the years. She was the one who told me I could find videos to make them online. I was in here, but I know about the bombs handcuffed to Officer Galloway and Agent Graves.

I also know that she made them."

"How do you know that? Did it have anything to do with your visitor?"

"It was the young man who told me. He told me a lot of things. I don't want anything to happen to him though. He's scared to death of Echo. She has his father and told him to do as she says or he would be the reason his father dies. What would you do in that situation? If it were me, I would do as I'm told. No one wants to be the reason for a family member to die. If we take a break in a few minutes I can try to get more information from him. He's supposed to see me again today. He told me I have to let her know when the police are close to finding her. To be honest, I just make stuff up. I will have him tell her that they are giving up on the search here in Brines and that the FBI thinks she has left town for good."

"We'll take a break and I'll have the agents look like they are packing up to leave town. Maybe it will help. Try to get any and all information you can from him. Tell him the police found you innocent of all charges and will be releasing you in about 48 hours. I'll see you after you are done."

I took the video over to the Chief's office and let him know what we discussed. The agents were told to pack up and as the boy entered the Chief announced that the investigation in Brines was over. Only a few agents would remain to watch Logan and me in case Echo returned.

The young man was led down to see Clara and the two were left alone to talk. Upstairs, Logan and I sat anxiously in the Chief's office. To make sure the young man didn't see us, we couldn't leave until he was gone, especially since Logan was in street clothes and not in uniform. The only good thing about being stuck in the small office was that they brought us some food. I could eat all day everyday if I wasn't honestly afraid of getting too fat. I may have joked about it, but it was not what I really wanted.

We were so afraid of the young man seeing or hearing us that we never spoke a word. After over an hour of silence, Chief Parks came in to let us know it was safe to come out. Logan and I went back into the interrogation room and prepared for the rest of the interview.

"I really hope she was able to get some answers for us. I'm so ready for this to be over," Logan stated with a half smile.

"I am beyond ready for normal to begin. This has gone on far too long."

Clara was brought in and had tears in her eyes. I couldn't help but feel bad for her and wondered what had made her so upset. Did Echo know our plan? Was she threatened in any way?

"What's wrong Clara? What was said to upset you so much?"

"I was just informed that Echo found a way into the hospital and killed my mother without anyone knowing she was there. He said she was blaming me for it because I was still talking to you. She thinks I told you where all of her hideouts are. If I keep talking to you she will kill the young man's father. I want her to pay, but I don't want her to kill anyone else. I don't know what to do."

"Do you know where any of her hideouts are?"

"The police can raid them immediately to lessen the chance of anything happening. We can hit all of them at once," Logan promised her. "I'm sorry for interrupting, but I wanted to let you know and try to ease your mind."

"What if they don't get there in time?" she cried further proving my theory.

"What if he's already dead and this is all a ploy to get you to keep quiet so she can keep on killing?" I asked hoping it would help.

Clara paused for a few minutes and her face went from sad to determined. "Let's do this. I want her to pay for what she did to my mom, the other people, you, and to me."

"Thank you Clara, I know this isn't easy for you. I know Echo scares you. I've seen it written all over your face. So why don't we start with any and all locations she has used in the past."

She nodded her head in agreement. "There is a small building outside of town that has a sign outside. It's a computer repair store. The sign is old and faded. It has a soundproof basement that she could use. To get into the basement you'll need to find the hatch hidden under the desk on the left. We used to go there when we were underage to drink and smoke pot. The land and building is still owned by her father."

"Make sure you write this down Logan. The agents will need detailed notes."

"The next building could be the old gas station on highway 63. The basement is not soundproof, but is large enough to torture and/or kill someone."

"Is there anything there they need to worry about when going in?"

"Yes, there is still a little bit of fuel in the tanks and she has explosives hooked up to them. She may blow them up as soon as she sees anyone there."

"That's a good thing to know. Would she blow it up if she's there?"

"I'm not sure if she would or not. She may do anything to keep from being caught. Echo herself is an unpredictable ticking time bomb. She may blow it up to make you think she killed herself."

"I understand. Where else could she be?"

"The only other places are one of her two houses and if my house has not been guarded, she could be there."

"Is that everything you can think of?"

"No, I just remembered one other place. Echo's father used to have a small plane at the airport. He moved his plane but kept the building in case he ever needed it. It also has a basement. It's where he kept all of his tools for working on the plane. Maybe she's there. Those are the only places I know of. Please tell the officers to be careful. I don't want any more people killed. Too many have died already and she needs to be stopped."

"I want to thank you Clara. I will personally make sure you have a guard at all times. We won't let anything happen to you. We will also have someone watching the young man so he does not get killed." Logan shook her hand.

We rushed out of the room and called a meeting in the Chief's office. The notes were handed over and arrangements were made to keep not only Logan and I safe, but also Clara and the young man being forced into helping Echo. It took two hours for the rest of the FBI team to come over from Springfield, Missouri and SWAT teams from Joplin and St. Charles to arrive.

Several plain clothes officers followed the young man and made sure he was safe. Homes near the old closed down gas station were evacuated just in case Echo decided to blow up the station. They also prepared a fake road crew to shut down the highway in front of it. Every precaution was taken including hidden officers and state troopers to watch all houses and buildings. Everyone wanted this to be over once and for all.

"Logan, I have butterflies in my stomach. Could it really be this close to being over? Are we really going to be safe and live a normal life?" I asked as I hugged him and placed my head on his chest.

"I hope so. If they don't catch her, we will have to go into the witness protection program. I don't want our child to be born and raised in that kind of life. I want to be home, safe, and happy. Whatever happens, I want you to remember that I love you." He kissed the top of my head.

"I love you too, and I'm so sorry I dragged you into this. If I had known it would turn out this way I never would have agreed to talk to Clara. It's all my fault for being so damn stubborn. Everyone told me not to do it, but I just wouldn't listen. Now several officers and my father are dead. You and Kim almost died, I almost died, and how many more will be lost or injured because of me? All because I couldn't let my mother's death go," I cried angrily into his chest.

"You can't blame yourself. You needed answers and you got them. Now they can catch Echo and lock her up for the rest of her miserable life."

"I don't know what I'll do if they don't find her."

As I finished my sentence the room started to fill with FBI agents and members of the two SWAT teams. I was asked to fill them in on all of the information I had and it was the most nerve wracking thing I ever had to do. Before I could finish my speech there was a loud explosion. We all paused for a moment. The teams stood to get ready for their searches as the young man who often came to talk to Clara walked back into the station. He was covered in blood and held a DVD case in his hand. He looked like he had seen a ghost and I was once again filled with fear. He dropped the disk on the ground and ran out the door.

A minute or two later we heard another explosion. It was followed by five more explosions each one a minute apart from the other. It was then that we realized she had set all of the buildings to explode and wanted the young man to blow up the police station. I knew in my gut that she was still alive and out there somewhere just waiting for me. The police chief and a few FBI agents were on the phone immediately trying to get help putting out the fires. The rest rushed out to try and help anyone who needed it.

I walked over slowly and picked up the case. Everyone was busy so I sat at Logan's desk and put the DVD in his computer. My hand started shaking as I hit play. As the sound of Echo's voice filled the room everyone went silent and many crowded around the desk to watch with me. It was a video of Echo and her confessions.

She had an ominous look on her face. "As you already know, I'm Echo Shay. I knew you would get close to finding me soon so I made this video and rigged all my known locations with bombs. The young man, Benny, was a spy who turned on me, so I had to get rid of him. If you're watching this, he failed at his final mission. I knew he was too weak, but that's beside the point. By the time you watch this I will be out of town. In fact, I will most likely be out of the state." She looked straight at the camera. "Don't worry Brooke, I haven't forgotten about you. I will find you one of these days. Right as you finally feel safe in your own home, I'll be there. Of course, you will have to find a new home or rebuild. That is if they don't find and deactivate the bomb by the time I have chosen to dial the number needed to blow it sky high." She let out a small chuckle of amusement.

"As for Logan, do you think you can get to your parents before I do? I've been looking for a couple to kill at the same time. Maybe I'll just wait and kill you when I kill Brooke. You'll find out soon enough."

I paused the video and Logan quickly dialed his parents hoping to get them somewhere safe. As he made the call to his parents, an FBI agent placed a call requesting that the Galloway's be taken to the FBI headquarters closest to them and kept there until it was safe.

"Hi Mom. Are you and Dad doing okay?" He tried to remain calm as he talked to his mom.

"Yes Logan. What's going on? The news said there were several explosions in Brines?" Her voice was shaky and he knew she was scared.

"Brooke and I are safe. There were seven explosions, but we weren't near any of them. FBI agents are on their way to get you and Dad. A threat was made on both of your lives. Do not answer the door, and pack just what you need. Call me when you're safe please."

"I don't understand why we were threatened."

"Echo can't get to Brooke or I so she may be after the two of you. She will do anything to get to us. Just promise me you'll stay safe."

"I promise I'll do whatever is needed to stay safe. I just hope they catch her soon. I love you Son. Give Brooke a hug for us and tell her not to worry."

"I love you too Mom. I'll try to keep her calm." He hung up the phone, but still wasn't smiling.

Once all calls were finished, and the few who left to help anyone who needed it were gone, I pressed play again.

"You can watch as I torture her in front of you. I'll make you listen to each other's screams as you beg me to end your lives. I thought I had made it clear that Brooke was to stop trying to get information she didn't need. Remember to always look over your shoulders." She grinned and it sent chills down my spine. "You'll never know when I may show up to end your lives. No one can save you now." The screen went black as she laughed.

All I could do was sit staring at the blank screen and cry. I tried to talk, but it was as if my voice had left me forever. Logan was brought a chair to sit in and everyone left in the room busied themselves with the tasks of trying to arrange a safe house for us, calling surrounding fire stations to help put out the fires and get people to safety, and sending the bomb squad to our house to search for the bomb. None of it felt real. Was I stuck in a nightmare, or was this my new reality? Maybe I should give up so she wouldn't hurt anyone else I loved. I didn't want to live in fear anymore. Too many people had been hurt or killed and I couldn't let it happen anymore. She killed her own sister trying to convince the police it was her. What if they never found her? I couldn't handle the thought of it. I was so full of fear, anger, and confusion that I barely made it reaching for the trash can under the desk, and almost puked all over myself, the floor, and the desk.

Logan cried as he rubbed my back and the feeling of dread settled into his bones. "Are you alright?"

"I think so," I whispered through my tears.

"I don't know how, but I promise you we will get through this. As long as we're together, we can make it. I don't want you stressing out. It's not good for the baby. Why don't you lay on the couch in the break room? I'll come get you when it's time to leave. Even if you can't sleep I at least want you to rest."

"I'll try and relax, but I make no promises." I slowly walked towards the break room. "I'm sorry about your trash can."

"It's fine Sweetie, just relax."

I sat on the couch too afraid to lie down. I couldn't let my guard down for even a second. We're no longer safe anywhere. In my mind no one could protect us anymore, not even the FBI. I cried for what seemed like hours until I finally fell into a deep sleep. My dreams were filled with the horrors I had lived through the last several months.

Chapter Seventeen

When I awoke, Logan was on the couch next to me, cradling me in his arms, and sleeping peacefully. I didn't want to wake him so I just laid there looking up at him for awhile. I was surprised by how relaxed he seemed, and if it weren't for feeling his body move with each breath he took, and hearing his heart beat, I would have thought he was dead. Not a thought I wanted to have. I forced a smile as I stared. Any other man would have broken my heart, left, and never looked back after the first incident. I couldn't believe how wonderful he truly was through all of this. When I finally looked out the window I noticed it was dark outside. They must have been having trouble finding a safe place for us. I carefully got up and went to find Chief Parks.

When I found him, he was watching the video again. He quickly paused it when he saw me standing in his doorway with a frown on my face.

"I'm sorry Brooke. I didn't see you come in. Did you sleep well?"

"Not really, but any sleep is good I suppose. Have they found anywhere safe for us?"

"Not yet, but they are trying. You'll have to leave the state."

"Did they find the bomb or is my house gone?"

"They found it about two hours ago. You're house is now bomb free. You will only get to go pack a few things, but not until they find somewhere safe for the two of you."

"I hope they hurry. I just want to get out of this town. I hate it here and I'm sorry I ever came back."

"This is not your fault. You did not make that woman a crazy psychopath. You had no idea that she was involved or that she would go bat shit crazy." He motioned for me to sit down, seeing that I was still very tired. "I sent an officer to the next town to get us all some food. Everything in this town is shut down for the time being. After you eat, if you want to, Clara is asking to speak to you. I told her you probably wouldn't want to see her ever again."

"It is fine, I guess. I still don't think she killed most or any of those people. Something just doesn't feel right. I hope we can get to the bottom of all this soon."

"Even in the worst situations you always try to find the good in others don't you?"

"If I can't believe in the good inside people, I have nothing left to cling to. The only person who has no good left in them is Echo. She is so full of hate and anger that it has taken her over completely. I can't imagine being that angry all of the time. Her life couldn't have been that bad. Could it?"

"I'm not familiar with her life and we haven't been able to locate any family members. I'm guessing she never got any help for her issues."

"Clara said she was constantly compared to her sister. She was also dumped on Clara's grandmother a lot when she was young. It's so sad to hear about a parent not caring for their own child."

"That must have been hard on her, but it's still no

excuse for killing so many innocent people. I wish there wasn't so much hate in this world. All we can do is try and help others overcome the hatred and anger they have inside. Let's go see if the food is here yet. I am starving tonight."

"That's a good idea, even though I hate to wake Logan."

We walked out of the office and headed for the break room. Logan was still asleep so I curled up next to him on the couch and waited for the officer to make it back with some food. Chief Parks and I continued to talk quietly and were joined by Kim and Ben after a few minutes. They tried to stay quiet so Logan could sleep and joined us in our conversation. We tried to talk about the things that made us happy instead of everything that had been happening. I talked about what my family use to do for Christmas and about what I pictured future Christmases would be like. As I talked about decorating the tree with Logan and our 4 children, he woke up and hugged me. It was nice to have plans, even if there was a possibility that they would never come true. I was still full of hope for the future.

"Good morning, or evening Logan," I said as I sat up to give him a kiss.

"Is it really morning? How long was I asleep?"

"Just a few hours or so," Chief Parks said as I shrugged my shoulders.

"I hope we didn't wake you?" Kim inquired with a half smile on her face.

"Just a little bit, but you are a loud mouth at times," Logan joked.

I hit Logan in the face with a pillow and stuck my tongue out at him. "Be nice or you don't get food if it ever gets here. I'll also withhold all kisses."

"I'm sorry Kim. You're not the loud mouth. Ben is." He

looked at me and smiled.

"I am not!" Ben shouted trying to play along.

"You guys are crazy. I just want to eat and get the hell out of Dodge. I want to feel safe again. I'm sure the whole town hates me by now for not stopping the interviews," I sighed.

Logan grabbed my chin and turned my head to face him. "I've told you a million times before. This is not your fault. Most likely, she would have done it even if you had stopped. Blaming yourself won't change anything. All we can do is move forward from here. Do you hear me?"

"I hear you, but nothing you say will change my mind or how I feel. I may not have made Echo a psychopath, but I did push her over the edge by trying to get information about my mother," I affirmed believing it with my whole heart.

Logan wrapped his arms around me and whispered in my ear. "I know you believe it, but that doesn't make it true. I love you always and forever, and I'll help you get through this. We can lean on each other. I love you with all of my heart and soul. Together we can help make this a better world for all four of our future children."

"I love you too, Logan. I know I can get past this with you by my side. You and this baby are the force to keep me going." I kissed him.

Finally, after almost an hour of waiting, the officer sent to get food showed up. No one knew what I would be craving so he got me five different meals. I was so hungry I ate three of them in the time it took the others to each eat one. As per usual, they all looked at me like I was crazy. It wasn't my fault I was so hungry. Well not entirely my fault. Logan was also to blame, but I was happy I had something wonderful to look forward to.

The last several months had been a whirlwind of crazy, and a flood of different emotions including meeting and falling in love with the most amazing man in the world. He was my husband, my rock, and the father of my unborn child. If changing everything meant not meeting him, I wouldn't change any of it no matter how painful it was to me. I was so happy to have him in my life even if I couldn't fully show it at the time.

We finished eating and went to find out if any plans had been made yet. I was anxious to get out of the small town I was once happy to call my home. As long as it wasn't some place colder and full of snow I was happy to go. I was secretly hoping for California or somewhere nice and warm. I could use some time to relax on the beach and work on my tan. This town was making me as pale as a ghost and I didn't like it. I wanted to be able to go out in public without being followed and sit in a restaurant to enjoy a meal without wondering if I was going to be killed. When the FBI director told us we would be going to Cocoa Beach, Florida, I was more than happy to go. It would be a good place to go and relax or go out and have some fun. Plus my favorite old show I used to watch with my parents was filmed there.

We were taken to our house to pack some clothes and a few essentials. We were told to take only what we had to have, but no phones, computers, tablets, or any electronics that could be traced. I did grab all of my flash drives with the interviews and my notes. If I was lucky I could work on writing a book. At least it would be something to do while in a new place. I wondered if I would get to choose my new name, or if they would pick one for me. Maybe I could pick an exotic name, or something rare. It was almost exciting to be someone else for a while. I also spent time thinking about what name I'd give Logan while I was packing. I smiled my first real smile as I finished packing. The agents refused to let me carry anything downstairs or to the car. I didn't mind since I was still so tired. They loaded everything into the car and we headed for the airport.

I slept on the way to Springfield, and Logan woke me up when we arrived. I felt like one of those movie stars with the car parked so close to the plane. This was new to me, but I guess when you're being whisked to a new home in an FBI private jet, you can do things like this. We said goodbye to Ben and Kim before boarding the plane.

It wasn't until right before takeoff that I remembered how sick I always got when flying. It was the reason I drove everywhere I went. My nerves kicked in and I lost all my dinner into several airplane sick bags. Logan had a sad look on his face, but he still couldn't help but laugh at me. As soon as we were allowed to move about the plane, an agent got me a Sprite. I thanked him and sipped it slowly. I fell asleep a half hour after takeoff with my Sprite still in my hand and spilled it all over myself before anyone realized I was no longer awake. Logan dried me off the best he could, then also fell asleep.

We slept until the plane landed and we were awakened and guided off the plane and to a waiting car. We sat quietly, half asleep, while we waited for our bags to be unloaded and placed in the trunk. An agent joined us in the backseat and gave us each an envelope with all of our new information in it. Included were our new drivers' licenses, social security cards, address, and other information we would need to start our new lives. It was scary and exciting to be somewhere new. This would be a new start at a life with no more looking over our shoulders.

When we arrived at the new house, we were met by an agent who would be staying with us for awhile. He was tall with dark brown hair and hazel eyes. He seemed familiar to me, but I just ignored it and went inside to check out where

I would be staying. He followed us in while introducing himself.

"Hello, my name is Lucas Taylor. I'll be staying with you while you're here in Florida." He reached out to shake our hands.

"It's nice to meet you Lucas. I'm Brooke, or was. I'm still confused. Do I use my new name even when I'm in the house or just when I'm out in public?"

"You will use your new identity at all times. It would be more confusing to switch back and forth, plus if you have the windows open other people may hear you."

"That makes sense. I'm Samantha and this is my husband Spencer. I guess we'll have plenty of time to get used to the new names. Now where do I unpack my clothes?"

"You'll have plenty of time. As for unpacking, your room is upstairs, the first door on the left. Why don't we sit and go over a few things before you do that."

"I guess I can wait. I could use something to drink though. It's been a very long day."

Lucas went to the kitchen and got me a glass of water. "Is this okay for now? I figured we could go shopping later as I didn't know what you liked."

"Water is good," Logan answered for me. "It will be odd to go to a store again. It's been awhile."

"I bet. So the first thing I need to tell you is that this is just a temporary stop for the two of you. This is not normal for the witness protection program. You must have friends in high places, but they thought the two of you could use a short vacation so you could relax. The two of you will only be here about a week. I'm under strict orders to basically be your tour guide, cook, and make sure you have fun. They are still finalizing your new safe house. This situation is tricky since they have no idea where Echo was heading. For the first month or so in your new place you will not be allowed to leave at all. I know it will be hard and stressful, but it's to ensure your safety."

"An entire month in the house without being able to go outside at all? I don't want to be a prisoner again," I whined like a child and pouted.

"Brooke! Crap this is difficult. Samantha, please stop whining. I don't like the idea either, but it may be the only way to keep us safe at first. Don't you want that? Would you rather go back home and live in fear every single day?" Logan looked at me with a sad look on his face.

"I know, I'm just ready for a normal life. I'm ready to go out in public and be myself. I'll behave," I lied knowing full well I wasn't going down without a fight.

"I don't believe a word you said. I know you won't behave. It's against your religion or something like that," Logan snickered.

"I can too behave. It's just not as fun," I grinned.

"Let's get you unpacked and to the store. I'm sure you're both hungry and we really don't have much food in the house. After that the two of you can go take a walk on the beach. Doesn't that sound better than arguing?" Lucas joked.

"I love that idea. I don't have a bathing suit though. We need to go shopping tomorrow. I want something cute to wear. You know before I get all fat from the pregnancy." We all laughed.

The trip to the store was fun. We ended up with more junk food than real food. I made the excuse that it was for the baby. "The baby can have anything it wants." Logan laughed but agreed to it so I wouldn't pout at him. We did however get some steaks to cook on the grill for dinner. I said no to baked potatoes and decided potato chips were a better idea. I did however agree to Logan's desire for shells and cheese. When we returned home, Lucas started the grill and I started the water boiling for the shells. I refused to let him keep me from cooking. It was, after all, something that made me very happy. I loved cooking for other people. Not enough to become a chef, but just for family and friends. We finally sat down for dinner and some conversation, but were too hungry to even start talking. It was the best meal I'd had in a long time. It was my first meal as a free woman.

Logan reached over and grabbed a chip off of my plate. "You weren't going to eat that one were you?"

I took the last bite of steak off of his plate. "You weren't going to eat that were you?"

"That's so rude. You don't steal a man's steak. Chips are fair game but red meat is not. You're so gonna pay for that one," he laughed.

"I'm pregnant so stealing any food off my plate is a big no-no. So now we're even." I stuck out my tongue.

"You two are too cute. Are you always like this, or is this something new?" Lucas piped in.

"We are only like this when we are happy. Don't get the two of us arguing. It could be disastrous. We could take out the whole town when we fight. Like Ironman vs. The Hulk. The whole town would be a goner," I said looking at Logan with a crooked smile on my face.

"That's putting itt mildly She-Hulk," Logan laughed.

Lucas cleared the table and gave us directions to the beach. He figured it would be safe for us to go alone this time. Not many people would be left on the beach and we could enjoy the sunset alone. I was thankful he didn't want to join us. Something still bothered me and I had the feeling we were being watched. Maybe agents were following us and we just didn't see them.

"You don't think Echo will find us here do you?" I whispered.

"No Sweetie. I think we are safe. Besides there are agents all over the place watching to make sure nothing happens. Echo is thousands of miles away. They will catch her soon and we will be able to go home and be safe." He wrapped his arms around me as we got to the beach.

"I've never been to the beach before. I think it's fitting that the first time I'm here I'm with my new husband. I love you Log…. I mean Spencer. You are the rock that keeps me going."

"This is my first time at the beach also. I'm glad I get to share this experience with you. It makes it that much better. Tomorrow we can go for a swim. Tonight let's just sit and watch the sun set together."

We sat on the beach wrapped in each other's arms, watching the sun sink into the ocean. It was such an amazing time. I must have fallen asleep in his arms, because when I awoke the next morning, I couldn't remember getting back home and in bed. I wanted to stay in bed all day. It was a perfect morning full of love and warmth. Not just warmth from the heat outside, but the warmth of love and knowing that at least for now we were safe and free to be ourselves again. I wanted nothing more than to stay in bed forever, but someone set an alarm and it was on Logan's side of the bed. I tried to crawl over him to turn it off, but he stopped me with a kiss. We spent the next hour in bed making love and enjoying the freedom we had both been longing for. In fact if Lucas had not walked in on us, we might never have made it out of that bed.

I walked to the kitchen to get some water and found myself too embarrassed to even look at Lucas. No one but Logan had ever seen me like that. It was not a good thing in my eyes. I mean who walks into a married couple's room without even knocking on the door? Was he some kind of pervert or something? Logan was going to have to talk to Lucas. I grabbed my water and went back up to my room to prepare for the day. Logan was already in the shower so I joined him. It was the longest non-shower I had ever taken. When we finally emerged from our room, Logan went straight for Lucas and pulled him aside for a little chat.

"Have you ever heard of knocking man?" Logan said a little too loudly.

"I'm sorry. You said you wanted to be up by a certain time and I figured you turned off the alarm and went back to sleep," Lucas admitted.

"You still need to knock. It's not cool that you just walked right on in. Then, instead of saying you were sorry and leaving, you stood there like it was some sort of show. Next time I'll kick your ass. Are we clear?"

"I got it. No more entering without knocking. It will never happen again. She does have a nice ass though," Lucas said as he took off running knowing Logan would hurt him for the comment.

"Just let him go sweetheart. We'll deal with him later. I want to go shopping. I need to find a cute bathing suit so we can go swimming. Let's go without him. We can handle that on our own." I grabbed his hand and led him out the door.

"I like the way you think. No wonder I fell in love with you. When all of this is over, will you marry me again? This time we'll have a big wedding with everyone there."

"Of course I will. I will marry you everyday if that's what you want."

"What do you mean if I want? Don't you want that too?"

"No, I just want every day to be a honeymoon. That, I could go for." I winked as we crossed the street.

We finally made it to a store where I could try on bathing suits. I went for the one piece suits, and he went straight for the two piece sets. So typical of a man.

"Honey, what size suit am I looking for?"

"I don't remember. Big on top and small on the bottom?"

He picked out a few and I went in to try them on. He waited outside for me to show them, but most did not fit right so I refused to come out. I opened the door a crack and told him to get me a top in a size bigger. He tried to peek in but I slammed the door shut. A few moments later he came back with not only the top but three more suits in the same size. I laughed as he tossed them over the door at me. It was so cute how interested in bathing suit shopping he was. Maybe I should have been nervous. Then I thought about that morning and knew I had nothing to be worried about. I tried on the last one and came out to show it off. He just stared at me with his bottom jaw dropped.

"WOW! You look absolutely amazing. Can we just make this your everyday wear?"

"I don't look too fat in it?"

"You'll never look fat in anything. Let's get that one and some towels then hit the beach."

We browsed the towels, and then picked out some flip flops. The walk home was nice, but I still had the feeling of being watched. Not in a good way either. Upon my insistence we walked home quickly and went straight for our room. We were stopped in the hall by Lucas who did not look happy in the slightest.

"And where did the two of you go? You know you still need to be followed for safety," Lucas said tapping his foot and placing his hands on his hips.

"You're an ass and I wanted to get away from you, so we went shopping. Now move out of my way so I can get ready to relax on the beach," I snapped.

"Someone took a grouchy pill today or is it just the hormones?" he said half joking.

Seeing the anger in my eyes, Logan stepped in front of me and pushed Lucas out of our way. "I'll deal with you later."

I took a little too long to get changed which left Logan plenty of time to make a phone call regarding Lucas's behavior that day. He made sure to let them know that if he wasn't replaced, Lucas might end up getting his ass kicked by a pregnant woman. That would look bad on the FBI when I wrote about it in my book. They agreed, but said there was no one else who could make it there for a few days. They promised a report would be put in his file and he would be reprimanded appropriately. Logan thanked them and started to get ready for the beach.

We finished getting ready and spent the rest of the day either on the beach or in the water. I didn't like the salt in the water but I loved being in the water and spending time feeling the sun on my skin. When the sun started to set we walked back to the house to shower and get ready for dinner. Neither of us was in the mood to cook, nor did we want to spend much time alone in the house with Lucas. We settled on a local restaurant off the beach where they had a live band playing. It was an all around great night. Afterwards we went home to sleep.

The next day was pretty boring, but we enjoyed it. We lounged around watching movies and pigging out on junk food. After we watched our third movie, Logan and I decided to head back to the beach. When I got up to leave the room I noticed Lucas staring at me. It made me feel uncomfortable so I decided to confront him.

"Is there a reason you're staring at me, or are you looking to get punched in the face?"

"I was just admiring your beauty is all. Is there something wrong with that?"

"When you're staring at a married woman it's a problem. Find someone else to stare at. Do you hear me?" I yelled.

"What's crawled up your ass today? Did someone wake up on the wrong side of the bed, or were you up all night realizing that there's a better man out there for you?"

"I've had enough of your bullshit Lucas. I'd rather deal with Echo coming after me than your dumbass." I turned to walk away and felt his eyes on me again. I turned around and punched him as hard as I could in the face. "I said stop staring at me, you fucking pig."

Logan who had been standing by in case he was needed was shocked at what I had just done. He lightly grabbed my arm and led me upstairs. We sat on the bed, not talking, and I noticed a smile on his face. I could tell he was proud of me for standing up for myself. I had to admit that it felt good to punch Lucas in the face.

I looked over at him and frowned. "Spencer, I don't feel like going to the beach. I'm gonna take a short nap first. Is that okay?"

"Hey, you remembered my name," he smiled. "That's ok Sweetie. I'll take a nap also. The beach will still be there later. I promise it won't get up and walk away."

We both felt unusually tired and I had a feeling something was wrong. I remember waking to a noise in the room late at night and seeing a dark figure standing next to the bed. Before I could scream or even try to wake Logan up, I felt a sharp pain on my head as I was hit with a large metal object.

TO BE CONTINUED

Acknowledgements And Back Story

Nightmare in the Shadows started as just a dream for me. I never thought I could ever write a book. I embarked on the adventure of a lifetime. I wrote this book as my story for my first ever NaNoWriMo.

I pledged to write 50,000 words in the month of November. When I got frustrated or stuck, my father was there with the push I needed to keep going. It was a success. Thank you Dad for keeping me going, and always making sure I knew I could finish. Your support means the world to me. You're the best friend anyone could ask for. I love you forever.

Echo Shea, what can I say? We met online at an event, and became instant friends. You are creative, wonderful, and so sweet. I love our chats we have late into the night. You always support me, and I am blessed to know you. Thank you for everything you have done for me. I hope you love the character who shares your name. You inspire me to be a better me.

I need to thank my amazing editors for making sure I publish the best version of the book possible. Aunt Jimmilee you are so amazing. I'm sorry you had to skip some scenes and I thank you for your hard work and dedication. You did an amazing job. Also, thank you Dad for picking up the scenes she was unable to read. Between the two of you, I know my book is amazing. I love you both.

To my beta readers: I know some could not finish on time due to health, or other issues, but I love you all. Without you my book would only be a shell. Your help is more important than you know. I send a great big hug to Andrew Sebastian Redden, Kandie Skinner, Michele Veronica Chudnofsky, and Teresa Baldwin - you are all superheroes in my book.

I would also like to thank my readers. I not only write for myself; I also write for you. Without you I'd have no one to share my stories with. I hope you enjoy the book.

Last, but not least I would like to thank all of the many authors who have inspired me and supported me through my writing process. To know I have the support of so many amazing authors is surreal. I truly believe authors should stand together and help lift each other up. I'm sorry for not mentioning your names, but there are far too many to add. I will always be there to support you with all of your future adventures. Thank you so much for everything.

About The Author

Stephanie Brown loved writing from an early age. In fourth grade she won a blue ribbon award for a school writing contest. After that writing was her favorite thing. She wrote poems every chance she had.

As Stephanie got older she dreamed of writing more than just poems, and wanted to write books for everyone to enjoy. After high school she started writing adventures for her friends and gaming group on a weekly basis.

She got her first serious writing job in 2015 when a close friend asked her to write a short story that would be included in an anthology. Her first work was published on Jan. 10, 2016 in The Lunch Time Anthologies: Gable Heights.

In November 2015 Stephanie took the leap and embarked on the journey of a lifetime. Through encouragement of one of her best friends, she started her first full length novel and finished it all for NaNoWriMo. It was the beginning of a wonderful journey.

She also enjoys reading and doing whatever she can to support fellow aspiring authors by encouraging them daily, and is also a proud supporter of indie authors. Stephanie hopes that someday her books will be known worldwide.

Follow Stephanie at:

www.facebook.com/AuthorStephanieBrown

http://www.twitter.com/AuthorSBrown

http://www.Stephanie-Brown.com